DESPERATE CHOICES

A BAD KARMA SPECIAL OPS NOVELLA

TRACY BRODY

Desperate Choices

ISBN: 978-1-952187-01-8

First edition

February 2020

Also available as an ebook

ISBN: 978-1-952187-00-1

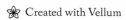 Created with Vellum

To my awesome and supportive husband and family.

PRAISE FOR TRACY BRODY

"Seat of the pants action with true military insight!" — Robin Perini, *Publisher's Weekly* Bestseller.

"You're going to love this Army Special Operations Team and Tracy Brody's authentic stories." — Angi Morgan, *USA Today* and *Publisher's Weekly* Bestseller.

"I loved this steamy and suspenseful prequel and can't wait for the rest of Brody's Bad Karma Special Ops series!" — Serena Bell, *USA Today* bestselling author of the *Returning Home* series

"It's a great romantic suspense story and I highly recommend it!" — Donna, Booksprouts Reviewer

I love Tracy's writing style and voice (and that her heroine is just as kick-ass as the hero!) — Christina Hovland on *Deadly Aim*

ONE

pril 2005

"Hey, Dolph!"

Ray's head jerked, and he grumbled under his breath at the high school nickname he'd despised.

He recognized the voice. But Stephanie Laakso—no, she was Anderson now—had never called him that. Why now? He placed two of his parents' dining room chairs in the bed of his truck and turned to see Stephanie crossing the neighbors' lawns, heading toward him with purpose. She balanced her toddler on her hip and motioned for him with her free arm.

"Hey. How's it going?" The car in front of her house was still there, and behind her, two men stood in her driveway. He eyed them as he strolled toward Stephanie. Both wore tan chinos, long-sleeved dress shirts, and ties, and the redheaded one wore a suit jacket. Their hands were empty

—no products for sale or visible Bible tracts—though they could be there to share their faith. He lengthened his stride as they started to follow her.

"Can you help me?"

The way she exaggerated "help me" and her wide-eyed expression stole Ray's focus from the wisps of naturally blonde hair framing her face. "What do you need?"

Alexis stared up at him and began to cry, probably intimidated by his height.

"I hate to impose, but could you and Emily watch Alexis for me again for a few hours tonight?"

The slight shake of her head contradicted her words.

"These detectives"—she jerked her head, appearing startled they stood a few feet away—"need me to come to the station regarding Sam's murder."

Emily? Why would Stephanie bring up his high school girlfriend? She wasn't making any sense, yet her sky-blue eyes stayed locked on his. Another look at the detectives and things clicked into place. Detectives who wanted her to come in at nearly seven o'clock at night didn't add up. Sam was killed eight months ago, about a month after Ray's two-week leave from Iraq. Not likely there'd be a time-sensitive break in the case now. His body tensed the same as if he heard an incoming mortar siren. He thought quickly. "I wish we could help, but I have to finish loading this furniture and, uh, deliver it tonight." He stopped before saying names or places. If Stephanie avoided using his real name, she could have a reason.

"I understand." Relief flashed across her face. "Do you have a minute to help me with something in the house, though?"

"Sure." He wasn't leaving her side with these goons here.

She turned to face the detectives. "Sorry. I really need to feed my daughter and get her in bed. I can come by in the morning before work. Should I ask for one of you or Detective Boothe?"

The thinner detective with limp brown hair hesitated. Ray added another inch of intimidation by raising on the balls of his feet. Alexis cried harder, and the man cowered. "Detective Boothe is out this week."

"Okay. Can I get your card?" Stephanie asked.

"Uh, no need. Ask for either of us." The detectives started to back away.

"You said you're Detective Wiesner, and you're Detective Farmer?" She motioned from the thinner guy to the redhead.

"Yes, ma'am. We'll see you in the morning." Wiesner nodded to a grumpy-looking Farmer, who cast one more chilling glance at Stephanie before he followed.

While Stephanie opened the trunk of her car, Ray watched the men pull away before he grabbed the groceries and carried them inside.

"You want to tell me what that was about?" He set the bags on the kitchen table. "Because I'd bet a month's pay those men were not detectives." Spotting an envelope and pen on the counter, he wrote down the vehicle's license plate number.

Stephanie exhaled audibly, shaking her head. "Thank you. I didn't think so either."

"Smart not using my name. Is that why you asked for their cards?"

"Partly. And I could swear the first time he said his name was Wieser, not Wiesner. *Liar*," she muttered. She placed Alexis in the high chair and fastened her in. "Them showing up without calling and wanting me to come down to the station didn't make sense even *if* Detective Boothe is out of town." She filled a sippy cup with milk, then handed it to Alexis. The child quieted, and Stephanie turned on the stove and slid a cast-iron skillet over the burner.

"Did they show you badges?" Those could be faked, though. He unloaded the bags while Stephanie removed the top from the container of rotisserie chicken and kept working.

"As a matter of fact, they did not." Now she growled, though it wasn't an overly threatening sound coming from her.

"Didn't think so. They had regular tags instead of permanent license plates for official state vehicles, too." He was pretty sure the police departments around Fort Campbell had permanent tags, but Taylors was a small town, and maybe South Carolina did things differently.

"I didn't even ..." She absently tucked a free strand of hair behind her ear, then began cutting up the chicken with shaky hands.

"Let me do that." He touched a finger to her hand, afraid she'd slice something other than the chicken. She let him take the knife. "Is this Detective Boothe the one investigating Sam's death?"

"Yes. He's had the lead since the beginning." She picked up the package of tortillas and bag of shredded cheese and assembled a quesadilla in the skillet. "Considering what I told him about last week, I think he'd be the one to contact me if he learned anything."

"What did you tell him last week?"

She looked at him and hesitated before asking, "How much did you hear about Sam's murder?"

"That he was found shot in the lot at Floyd's Fine

Motors. My dad said they thought it was attempted robbery or someone trying to boost a car."

Stephanie nodded. "They didn't have much to go on. The security cameras were not working, so there wasn't any video and no leads. But I stopped back at the dealership one night last week ..."

"Wait. You're still working there?"

"Yeah." She cut the quesadilla and took a nibble before placing a triangle on the high chair tray. "The owner, Gary Floyd, was shook up after it happened and offered to give me a recommendation, but I was a wreck and couldn't deal with taking care of Alexis and trying to find and learn a new job."

Ray couldn't imagine working at the same place where her husband was killed but kept his mouth shut. She didn't need him pointing that out when she dealt with it every day.

"The part-time receptionist who helped with the title work did quit. Gary decided not to replace her, saying I could do both jobs, and he'd pay me more. Only it's enough additional work that I have trouble getting it all done. On Wednesdays, Gary leaves at five, so my friend Renee, who works at the day care, takes Alexis home with her, and I stay late to catch up." She assembled another quesadilla. "Last week, I heard a car pull in as I was about to leave. With what happened to Sam, it made me nervous, so I took my phone with me in case I had to call the police and peeked out. I saw a guy get something from one of the cars that had come in that day. I couldn't help but wonder if it could be related to Sam's murder."

Ray's mind had gone there, too. "Did you see what he got out of the car?"

"No. It might have been wrapped in a bag, but it wasn't

big. I tried to get a picture of the guy but only got his back before he got in his car and left. I debated whether to tell Gary because I didn't want him knowing I stayed late and thinking I can't keep up. I really need this job. But I had to say something. Gary seemed more focused on why I was there, but when I told him, he said the guy who drove the transport carrier had left something in the car. He said he left the car unlocked—which would explain how the guy got in without breaking a window."

"But ..." Ray picked up on her hesitation.

"Something felt off. So I did a little digging. You want a quesadilla?" she offered.

"No." He wanted the rest of the story.

"Gary buys about half his inventory from bigger dealers and auto auctions. That day we'd had two cars delivered. One of the vehicles came from a dealer in Miami that he buys from regularly. At least once a month. It got my brain spinning with ideas."

"Whoa." What were the chances that was purely coincidental? Slim to absolutely none would be his guess.

"I called Detective Boothe and told him, and he thought it sounded suspicious and was going to contact the local authorities in Miami to see what they could tell him about the dealership there. I haven't heard from him yet."

"You should call him to check these guys out."

"Good idea." She turned off the burner, then plucked a business card from the wire letter holder next to the phone on the counter. After about thirty seconds, she gave an exasperated sigh.

Ray waited until she'd left a message. "He probably won't get that tonight. Why don't you call the station and ask for those detectives?"

She nodded and dialed again while Alexis slurped

down milk. "Yes, I'd like to speak to Detective Wieser, or maybe it's Wiesner. He's not. Is Detective Farmer in? Can you transfer me to his voice mail, please?" Her face scrunched while listening before she hung up. "I couldn't tell if that was Farmer's voice because he didn't say much, but the names check out. Maybe I'm being paranoid," she conceded.

"I'm not convinced you are, and until you talk to Detective Boothe, you can't stay here."

"I don't have anywhere to go," she interrupted him.

"If they aren't legit, they could come back. It's not safe for you or Alexis. You can stay at Mom and Dad's new condo."

"I can't impose on them."

"It's not up for debate. Pack what you need for a day or two for you both." He drilled her with the intense stare he'd developed as second-in-command in junior ROTC, hoping it'd work.

She met his gaze head-on before the trace of defiance in her eyes fled. Her shoulders sagged, and she stroked Alexis's curls, which were nearly the same champagne shade of blonde as her own. "Okay. Thank you."

He caught the shimmer of moisture in her eyes before she checked and removed the second quesadilla from the pan. It evoked a desire to take her in his arms and assure her that she'd be safe. That she didn't have to face this alone.

Stephanie took a bite of a quesadilla and handed Alexis another piece. "Can you keep an eye on her while I throw some stuff in a bag?"

"O-kay." Why did overseeing one toddler for a few minutes stir up more fear than doing door-to-door searches for insurgents in Iraq?

"I'm right down the hall if you need me."

Stephanie must have picked up on his hesitation, based on the amused grin she shot him. It was worth it to see her smile though, even if only for a second.

Once she disappeared, he surveyed the kitchen. In high school, he'd spent as much time here, hanging out with her brother Niklas, as his own house. Stephanie and Sam moved in after her dad's promotion took her parents back to Finland, and the house had hardly changed. Now he looked around through the eyes of a combat veteran. With the little Stephanie had told him, he'd already concluded that the men were on the other side of the law, trafficking illegal drugs. If they weren't detectives, they wouldn't come back during daylight. This was typically a safe street. The neighbors kept the front lights on, and the older houses were close together. If he wanted to break in, he wouldn't risk coming in the front door. The back door, though ...

He stepped over and checked the door that entered into the kitchen. No security alarm panel. In addition to the simple doorknob lock—that would take all of twenty seconds to pick or force—there was a deadbolt. Still, that wouldn't keep out the wrong kind of people. They could bust a windowpane on the door, or the side window, or even a bedroom window in a matter of seconds. She was not staying here. But this was her home now, and she couldn't stay away indefinitely. He needed a plan.

Alexis banged her empty cup on the tray.

"You want more?" he asked, though several pieces of her dinner remained.

"Ma-ma-ma," she said and pushed away some of the food, then rubbed a fist over her eye.

It took him a minute to figure out how to release the tray from the high chair. When he tried to lift her, he met with resistance, then found the strap holding her in. Once he unfastened it, he carried Alexis down the hallway. Stephanie was in her childhood bedroom, which now held a crib, rocking chair, and small dresser. She packed diapers into a fashionable backpack.

"Do you have a video camera?"

She looked up from her task. "Yeah. We bought a used one so we could send videos of Alexis to my parents and grandparents in Finland and Sam's mom, dad, and stepmom in Nebraska. Why?"

"I'm going to set it up in case you have visitors tonight."

"It's in the coat closet. Top shelf." She took Alexis from him, worry clear in her eyes.

After he retrieved the black bag, he laid the contents on the kitchen table and took inventory. The player was nice and compact. He rewound the tape and pressed play. As he expected, the scene that played was of Alexis. Her laughter as she went down a small, colorful slide made him smile. Her innocence reminded him of why he'd dropped out of college to join the Army shortly after 9/11. Someone had to fight evil in the world. Joining up had been his plan for years, but after watching the towers fall, he wasn't waiting three more years to graduate.

He let the little girl's laughter seep into his core. No way was anyone hurting her or Stephanie on his watch. He left the video playing while he removed the cellophane wrap from an unopened tape. After he replaced the tape, he set aside the one Stephanie would want to keep.

Stephanie's voice carried down the hall in that animated way adults talked to babies, little kids, and animals. Ray checked the amount of charge on the main camcorder battery, then swapped it for the spare. After he plugged in the charger, he skimmed through the owner's manual and adjusted the settings for the longest play. Six hours. Still not long enough. And he couldn't count on the max battery life with an older recorder. He needed a backup plan to cover the whole night and going forward.

Okay. Where to put it? The top of the fridge would be stable and had a clear line of sight to the door. However, people doing something shady tended to keep their heads down. He needed a face shot of anyone who came in. The kitchen counter was too obvious. Unless ...

Rummaging in the cupboards, he found a cracker box and held it next to the camera. He took the package out and slid the camera in. Perfect fit.

TWO

"It's going to be okay, sweetie," Stephanie crooned to Alexis, but said it more to calm her jangling nerves as she got Alexis ready for bed. The guilt about dragging Ray into this was assuaged by the need to protect her daughter after the two detectives ramped up their insistence that she come down to the station tonight.

They hadn't solved Sam's murder in eight months. Why the sudden urgency? If it had been Detective Boothe, he would have called. Still, if he'd been here, she probably wouldn't have thought twice about going with him. Ray's doubts about the detectives, too, reassured her she wasn't totally paranoid, but his concurrence scared her all the more.

What if the man she saw at the dealership killed Sam or was tied to who had? The way he'd checked out the area and kept his head down hadn't been the typical actions of a person with honest intentions. She should have made a copy of the security recording for Detective Boothe, but by now, it was recorded over. If only she'd gone with her gut before telling Gary what she'd seen. Police had looked into everyone at the dealership and found nothing suspicious, but could Gary be involved? She didn't want to believe he'd do anything shady—especially murder—but now she analyzed everything through suspicious eyes. Was the extra work he gave her an attempt to get her to quit?

When she'd started the job, Gary treated her like the stereotypical dumb blonde, especially since she hadn't stayed in college. She'd tolerated his occasional condescension, and in nearly three years now of working at Floyd's Fine Motors, she'd proved she was more than a pretty face. Maybe too smart for her own good since, lately, life was making her take off her rose-colored glasses—and she didn't like the shadows she was seeing.

She tugged the pink pajama top over Alexis's head of curls and pressed a kiss to her forehead. "Momma will do whatever it takes to protect you, sweet girl."

She was close to her younger siblings, Nik and Anni, but they were both in college here in South Carolina. Beyond sending gifts to Alexis and offering emotional support, they weren't in a position to help, at least until Anni came home for the summer. Mom had stayed two weeks after Dad returned to Finland following Sam's funeral, and Stephanie briefly considered moving back to Finland herself. It'd be nice to have her parent's support, and she could help with her aging grandparents, but her friends were here. Sam's parents weren't nearby, but they'd likely never make it to Finland to see Alexis.

The past eight months had been a struggle. She'd made it through with help from friends and neighbors like the Lundgrens, but Ray's presence gave her the most comfort she'd experienced since Sam's death.

In the kitchen, she found Ray cutting a hole in the graham cracker box. "What are you doing?" She let go of the suitcase to grab a box of macaroni and cheese to bring for Alexis.

"Camouflage. On the chance those two make a repeat appearance, I don't want them taking off with the evidence." He slid the camcorder inside the box. "Stand over by the door for a minute."

She did as instructed, despite the uneasy churning in her stomach again. Ray set the box on the counter next to the canister set and marked the angle by drawing lines on a piece of paper.

"Thanks. Let me check this, and we'll be ready to go."

She packed yogurt cups and a few more food items in a lunch cooler while he viewed the playback on the video recorder, then repositioned it.

Ray checked that the door was locked, and without asking, took her suitcase to the front door. Before leading her out, he peered up and down the street, then waited while she locked the deadbolt.

"We're going to take my truck," he instructed when she headed for her car.

"I'll need the car seat," she said, putting Alexis down to unlock the car. She unfastened the seat and wrestled it out with Alexis clinging to her leg.

"I got that." Ray hefted the heavy seat as if it were a bag of chips.

Stephanie scooped Alexis up and hurried after him.

"Um, I'll let you do this," he said, setting the seat in the narrow space behind the passenger seat.

She squeezed in and threaded the seat belt to secure the car seat while Ray stowed her suitcase in the truck bed between the dining room chairs.

"Be back in a minute," he called and disappeared into his parents' house. He returned with two more chairs.

"Can you hand Alexis up to me?"

Alexis didn't fuss when he picked her up this time. Stephanie buckled her in while Ray secured the chairs with straps, then he closed the tailgate with a solid, metallic *thunk.*

Sitting in the cab next to Ray as he drove down the street where she'd grown up brought back memories. This truck was nicer than the old one he'd driven in high school. It had clean, plush bucket seats and automatic windows. A GPS unit was plugged into the cigarette lighter. On the rare occasion she'd ridden somewhere with Ray and Nik when they had been in high school, she'd get wedged between them on the bench seat—shoulder to shoulder and thigh to thigh with Ray. Her skin heated as the memory flooded her mind. Even when Ray dated Emily Ferguson for a year and a half, no other boys appealed enough to her to date. After Ray left for college, she'd carried that torch until she met Sam.

When Ray came to her and Alexis's aid, that old flame flared like a match tossed on seasoned wood. It's just loneliness and his calming presence. *Now isn't the time. I'm a single mom in a jam, and he's helping because I'm his best friend's older sister, and he's a brave soldier. Don't start getting crazy ideas again.* She couldn't tell if this was Nik's voice or her own, after her brother brain-washed her with repeated admonitions that his best friend would never date a boring bookworm like her. Still, Nik hadn't managed to kill her crush on the boy almost next door.

"I know this is a little late, but welcome back from Iraq. Sorry I didn't do a better job of sending care packages and writing while you were deployed."

"Don't apologize. You had a lot to deal with. You sent

more than most people, and those brownies were freaking awesome. Made me the most popular guy in the company."

"Thanks for your letter. It meant a lot." She didn't tell him that it'd surprised her to get it.

"Over there, you hear about people getting shot and killed all the time, but this happening here ... To you—well, your husband—I wasn't sure what to say, but I wanted to send my condolences."

"I'm glad you came home safely," she said to let him off the hook before it got too awkward. "Are you planning to stay in or go back to college after you serve your four years?"

"Staying in. My parents wanted me to finish college and enter as an officer, but college really wasn't my thing. I didn't like being told to take required classes I'll never use versus taking classes on things I want. My Spanish isn't bad, and I'm learning Arabic, too."

"Makes sense. Real-life experience can be more educational than attending fraternity parties and nearly flunking out."

"Nik got his sh—act together." Ray shot a glance at Alexis in the back seat.

"Yes. Taking a year off to work retail taught him what he didn't want to do for the rest of his life. He'll graduate with his engineering degree *and* masters next year and hopes to get an offer from the company he interned with last summer."

"He mentioned that. Sounds like we both found our place."

Stephanie nodded. Nik had stumbled a little but recovered. She, on the other hand, didn't have it figured out—at least not anymore. Being married and a mother had been her dream. Just like her mom. Working at the used car dealership was a decent way to support herself, but it had never

been her long-term plan. Of course, being widowed with a
toddler hadn't been in her plans either. The idea that
because she worked there, someone might want to harm her
or her daughter sapped the last of her emotional reserves. If
it wasn't for Ray stepping outside to load the furniture, she
didn't know what would have happened.

When they got to his parents' new condo on the lake
fifteen minutes away, Ray let her pull the suitcase and carry
Alexis while he managed two dining room chairs in one
trip.

"There you are. I was starting to—" Mr. Lundgren
stopped, his gaze taking in Stephanie, Alexis, and the suitcase. "Stephanie, hi. I ..."

Ray's mother peeked around the corner, then stepped
into the foyer. Her face conveyed her surprise.

"They need to stay here tonight." Ray set the chairs
down in the dining room off the foyer of the modern, open-
concept condo.

"We're still unpacking and—"

"It's not safe for them at her house." Ray cut off his
mother's protest. "Two men showed up at her house that we
need to check out with the detective working Sam's murder
case."

"Oh, dear." Her expression morphed into motherly
concern. "Of course, you're welcome. This way. Excuse the
boxes." She motioned for Stephanie to follow.

"We'll bring up the rest of the chairs." Ray signaled his
dad with a jerk of the head.

In one of the bedrooms, a queen-size bed was made up.
A dresser filled the space between the windows. A camouflage duffel bag sat on top, and a mirror rested against the
front of it.

"Do you want Alexis in the bed, or would you rather I

find some blankets to make a bed on the floor?" Tarja Lund-gren asked.

"The bed is fine. I'm sorry to show up uninvited when you're settling in."

Mrs. Lundgren turned down the cover of the bed. "No need to apologize. You're like family, and if my son thinks you need to be here, you're welcome to stay as long as you need."

Stephanie eased Alexis's blanket from the diaper bag. Her daughter took it, snuggled into Stephanie's shoulder, and stuck her thumb in her mouth. "I'll tuck her in and be out in a minute."

"Do you need anything?"

"You letting us stay is enough." The answers and peace of mind she needed were beyond Tarja Lundgren's scope of duty.

Even in the unfamiliar location, Alexis settled in for bed without a fuss, closing her sleepy eyes. Stephanie slipped out of the room and followed the voices to where Ray talked to his parents.

"I'm going to need your keys," Ray said when she joined them.

"What for?" she hesitated.

"I'm going to stay at the house in case—"

"You can't do that. What if those two come back?" she said, despite Ray holding up a hand and trying to talk over her.

"I'm staying at Mom and Dad's. Not your house," he assured her. "I'll need to switch out the tape and battery on the camcorder. I won't do anything stupid. If I see anything, I'll call the police."

"Do you promise?"

"Yes." Ray didn't flinch under her scrutiny.

His parents nodded as if they'd warned him, too.

"My old bed's there, and I'll be back in the morning with another load of boxes."

Though his parents left the room as if reassured, she couldn't shake fear's cold grip on her. "You can go change the battery and tape, but you are not allowed to spend the night at my house, and that's an order." She drilled Ray with what she hoped was an authoritative stare. "I can't have something happen to someone else I care about."

"Order acknowledged."

The sympathetic look in Ray's blue eyes about did her in, and when he stroked her upper arm, she melted against his solid chest. His arms encircled her in a natural way that reassured her they'd get answers, and soon she'd be safe. Her arms slipped to his back and stayed there longer than they should, but she felt safe and good and right. Years ago, she'd dreamed of being close to him like this, but for different reasons.

"Thank you." She pulled back before she crossed the line of friendship. He was helping her out until she caught up with Detective Boothe, then he'd return to Kentucky or wherever the Army sent him next. No point in mooning over a man who'd never shown any romantic interest in her. He might have flirted with her after his family first moved in two doors down, or maybe that had been her hopeful imagination. Regardless, that had stopped after he'd met more girls, thanks in large part to hanging out with Nik all the time, and then the two of them had dated the Ferguson twins.

"I'll see you in the morning." Ray paused as if he wanted to kiss her. But he didn't and she wasn't daring enough to kiss him. Not now. Not years ago.

Back in high school, girls swooned over Ray. He was

hard to miss at over six foot four, with broad shoulders and a lean, athletic build. Add in his piercing blue eyes, golden blond hair that even made her jealous of its shade, and his shy smile, and she'd fallen hard, despite him being younger. It went beyond his looks. It was the way he talked to her and treated her that made her feel special. He still made her feel that way.

Women likely threw themselves at him even more now. He probably had a girlfriend, not that his parents had mentioned one. Though he'd been deployed to Iraq for nearly a year, it'd be easy enough to keep a relationship going by messaging. But she shouldn't let her mind go down the "what if" road. It'd only been eight months since Sam died. It's not like she was so desperate and horny that she needed to fantasize about her unrequited teenage crush. Still, she squeezed his hand before he headed out, leaving her emotions more jumbled than ever.

He DIDN'T HAVE to follow orders from Stephanie—did he? She was a civilian. Except experience proved that bad shit happened more often when you didn't follow direct orders than when you did. How many years had it been since Nik said his sister was off-limits? If it'd been anyone other than his best friend—the first friend he'd made after the move from Albuquerque to Taylors, South Carolina—he would have told them to fuck off. Instead, he kept things in the friend zone despite the way he occasionally caught Stephanie watching him, too.

Holding Stephanie back there stirred up all those old longings. Man, he hadn't wanted to let go. She felt so good. Smelled good, too. Kind of like honeysuckle. The aroma lingered in his memory. Damn, he needed to focus on his plan to make sure nothing happened to her or Alexis. If she'd stumbled across a drug trafficking operation, there was no telling how far someone might go to cover it up. He'd honor his promise and follow her orders, but that didn't mean he'd sit on his ass and do nothing.

He purchased four infrared motion detectors at the electronics store and by the time he got home, it was dark. Maybe the neighbors wouldn't see him set up the detectors around Stephanie's house, covering all four sides. Once they were in place and on, he tested the alert volume. That would wake him.

Inside her house, he checked the windows, turned on the front porch and foyer lights, and closed the bedroom doors, locking the master. He set the recorder and left the kitchen light on. That should help get a decent video if anyone came in. He might feel silly tomorrow if they found out those two were legit, but he had good instincts, and doing house-to-house searches for insurgents and weapons caches in Iraq had honed his ability to read people. His instincts had saved lives—his and his buddies'—and he'd rather be wrong about those detectives than be haunted forever if anything happened to Stephanie or Alexis.

He debated whether to set up a makeshift alarm using metal pots and ruled it out. It'd be better to give the cops more time to arrive in the event someone tripped the infrared alarm. Time to follow orders and go home. He'd either get a clue on how screwed Stephanie was or get a decent night's sleep and reassurances in the morning.

THREE

"I need you to get up." Ray's deep voice was soft near Stephanie's ear.

He rubbed her arm with his warm hand, rousing her from sleep. Was she dreaming? She forced her eyes open. Light streamed in from the hallway, and Ray's face was mere inches away. She raised her hand but stopped short of stroking his jawline.

"You'll want to get dressed. Detective Boothe is here with me."

"What? Why?" She jerked up onto an elbow. Behind her, Alexis cooed at the disturbance.

"I'll explain in the kitchen." He straightened and stepped out of the room, barely making a sound despite his size.

Stephanie slipped out from under the sheet, taking a moment to stare at Alexis. Her stomach cramped as she stripped off her camisole, then put on a bra and T-shirt. She didn't bother to brush her teeth or even her hair but hurried toward the low voices. The smell of coffee greeted her on her way to the kitchen.

"What happened?" She looked Ray over more closely in the light, then checked the clock. A little after five in the morning. Whatever was up couldn't be a good thing.

"You had visitors at the house."

"More like breaking and entering." Detective Boothe looked even more rumpled than usual with his button-down shirt half tucked in. He eyed the pot filling with coffee.

"Did you catch them?" Stephanie's heart pounded in her chest like someone had given her a shot of pure adrenaline.

"Afraid not. I set up an alarm using infrared motion detectors and called 9-1-1 when it went off. A patrol car was there in under seven minutes, but they were gone. Did get good video, and it's the same two who showed up at your house yesterday."

As quickly as her heart had revved up, it braked to a near halt. "How'd they get in?"

"Jimmied the window next to the kitchen table. Good thing you weren't there," Detective Boothe said. "Your friend here filled in the uniformed officers who called me at home."

"I'm sorry."

"Don't be." He shook off her apology about the middle-of-the-night call. "The men who broke in are not detectives with our department. We may be able to ID them from the video. This may be a break in the case. Good job."

"Did you find out anything about the auto auction company in Florida that Gary bought the cars through?"

"They checked out. Totally clean."

"You're sure?" She so wanted to be right about her theory. To get justice for Sam. That they were back to no leads, coupled with these fake detectives, was a frustrating step backward.

"Owners have a spotless reputation in the community down there."

Ray grumbled and removed the coffee pot to fill three mugs.

Stephanie wrapped her hands around the mug Ray gave her to ward off the chill seeping into her core.

"I still think you may be onto something." Detective Boothe took a sip of his coffee. "They transport those vehicles via carriers. Do you know if they use the same company or driver?"

That hadn't occurred to her. "I have no idea. I handle the financing documents, titles, payoffs, and verify insurance, but I don't deal with transportation logistics or payment. Gary pays those invoices."

"I'm thinking this could be a lot bigger than transporting drugs to one local dealer. What if they're using the carrier to deliver to several locations?"

"Does that mean you don't think the owner, this Gary, is involved?" Ray found the sugar canister in the pantry and placed it on the breakfast table.

"His story about knowing the transport driver was coming to pick up something he left in a car ..." Boothe snorted. "Now, two clowns showing up to talk to Mrs. Anderson a few days after she told him about seeing this guy?"

He shook his head, letting that set in before he continued. "After what you told me, I did some digging through his financials. His son was arrested for driving under the influence a few years ago. According to the arrest record, the kid was high as a kite when he crossed the center line into oncoming traffic." The detective's disdain came through loud and clear. "The woman he hit sued. They settled, but your boss mortgaged everything. Then, about two years ago, he started making regular cash deposits to a new account. All that's too coincidental for this old dog to buy him not being involved." He shot her an apologetic look and slurped down coffee.

Ray nodded in agreement. "Could anyone else at the dealership be involved?"

"Gary was the only one I told." Though she needed caffeine to think clearly after a few restless hours of sleep, she wasn't sure her stomach could handle it. "What now? I mean, I can't go back to work if—" If they wanted her to keep quiet. If they wanted her dead, too.

"If you don't, that could tip them off and make you more of a target. Right now, we only have speculation. There are no grounds to get a warrant. If I show up asking questions, they'll destroy any evidence. Remember how, *conveniently*, the surveillance system wasn't working when your husband was killed? Then they lie low, and we may never solve his murder."

"And there's no guarantee they leave *her* alone," Ray added.

The reality of how screwed she was no matter what she did shut down the part of her brain that controlled rational thought. She wanted justice for Sam, but Alexis was her priority. She couldn't risk her daughter becoming an orphan. If it weren't for Sam's parents, moving to Finland wasn't such a crazy idea. Her in-laws lived and worked in Nebraska, so it wasn't like they were close or able to help her. Her ability to speak Finnish was about that of a nine-year-old, the age she'd been when they moved to the States, but she'd pick it up. What kind of job could she get there, though? Her future was thrown into turmoil by Sam's death, but this chaotic turn might put her over the edge.

Both men remained silent as she took it all in. "You want me to go back to work?"

"I don't think that's—"

"Yes." Detective Boothe talked over Ray. "If you can get the name of the carrier service, see if it was the same one that made the delivery the day Sam was killed and again last week, even see if they have a drop-off scheduled, we can stake out the car. If we catch them smuggling illegal substances, we can bust them. Maybe shut down their operation. And keep you safe. It could also lead to finding out who killed your husband."

But that meant going back where they'd have easy access to her. "I don't know if I can do it. Wouldn't it be suspicious?"

"Not as much as suddenly quitting. Gary may think you've connected the dots back to him."

He had a point. "I need some time to think about it."

"I understand." The detective's words didn't quite pair with his disgruntled expression. "It's best if you call to say you won't be in today because of the break-in. You don't work weekends, do you?"

"No."

"Good. That'll buy us two more days."

"I can do that. What should I say, though?"

"We can work up a cover story Gary will buy."

Boothe likely directed her on the path he wanted her to take, but she had to trust he wouldn't put her life in danger —or *more* danger.

SUNLIGHT PEEKED through the kitchen window. After working through scenarios for nearly an hour and a pot of coffee, they had a story that sounded plausible and might even make Gary or whoever he was involved with call off the dogs. She wanted to record a message rather than talk to him. Less chance she'd slip up. But she caved to Detective Boothe's preference of calling Gary at home so he could listen in to gauge his reactions. Even though she'd role-played it with Ray, her whole body shook when she punched the numbers on the phone.

The first ring echoed loudly on speakerphone. Each subsequent ring raised her hopes it would go to voice mail.

"What the hell?" Gary answered, his voice thick with sleep.

"Gary? It's Stephanie."

"Stephanie? What time is it?"

"I'm sorry to call so early, but I won't be in today." She heard movement in the background. "Someone broke into my house last night." She paused as Detective Boothe instructed.

"Shi—Um, are you, uh, all right?"

Detective Boothe's eyes squinted, and his mouth twisted as he listened to Gary fumble for words.

"Shook up, but okay otherwise. I have to go to the police station to give a description of the two men who came to my house earlier in the evening." She focused on not giving too many specifics.

"Someone came to your house before the break-in?"

"They were here when I got home, claiming to be detectives. Except something felt off, and it seems pretty coincidental to have someone break in hours later." She picked up on Gary grumbling lowly as she talked.

"Do you have any idea what they wanted?"

"I think it's because I got a life insurance check this week. Maybe one of these guys was in the bank and overheard the teller say she needed to get the manager to approve the withdrawal on a large insurance check or saw her give me a good bit of cash. The police said they could get the video from the bank. I don't know how long all this will take."

"Don't worry about it. Take care of what you need to deal with. I'm glad you're okay."

"Thanks for understanding." She worked to keep sarcasm from leaching into her tone. How much was Gary involved? She clicked off and let the tension unfurl from its death grip on her core and flow to her limbs.

"You did good," Detective Boothe assured her.

Ray nodded as well. His gaze fixed on her in a way that made her want to be in his arms again.

"Once the crime scene guys finish processing your house, they'll let me know. I'll go over with you to inspect the damage, see if anything is missing. What about your daughter? Can you take her to day care?"

"I'll ask Mom to watch her this morning," Ray said. "Might be safer."

After they agreed, Ray went to wake his mother. Stephanie changed into the clothes she'd packed and dressed Alexis. By the time she returned to the kitchen, Tarja was cooking breakfast. Even Detective Boothe didn't dare try to leave before eating the oatmeal and eggs.

"What time are you leaving for Atlanta?" Ray asked his mom.

"Not until one or two. Are you ...?" Tarja trailed off.

"No. I need to stay. Give my regrets to Aunt Sanna and Uncle Jonas. Emma will be too busy to miss me."

"Don't miss the wedding on my account," Stephanie said. She never should have involved Ray. He'd just come back from a year in Iraq and came to town to see his parents and help them move before his cousin's wedding. Now she was messing up his entire trip.

"This takes priority," Ray said in his it's-non-negotiable tone.

Detective Boothe spooned more raisins onto his oatmeal. "Do you have a place you can stay for a few days? Give us a chance to ID and pick up those two?"

She had friends here, but she couldn't risk putting them in danger. Her parents were in Finland. Anni lived in a dorm, and Nik shared a two-bedroom, off-campus apartment with a roommate. Neither had room for her and a toddler. "Not really. I, uh ..."

"You can stay here," Tarja interjected.

"I can't impose like that."

"Nonsense. You're already here, and we'll be out of town until Sunday night. It's not an imposition."

"You aren't staying at your house alone." Ray's expression was pure, one hundred percent, I'm-not-budging-on-this. "Here makes more sense. They closed on the condo this week. No one would know to look for you here."

"I agree. This is a more untraceable option than staying with family or using a credit card to pay for a place."

The detective's take on it overcame any objection she could make. After staying strong for Alexis the past eight months, Stephanie was exhausted. She didn't want to be alone right now, and Ray's protective presence restored some peace of mind. If even for a few days for the police to look into who broke into her house, she'd take the reprieve.

FOUR

Ray made notes of supplies he needed to get at the hardware store after doing a security check of the house. Whoever had come made feeble attempts to stage it like a robbery.

Fortunately, other than the window they'd jimmied to get in, the only damage was a few drawers of clothes dumped in her bedroom and items knocked off the shelves in her closet. Detective Boothe left after going through the house with Stephanie to determine what, if anything, they'd taken, and she'd been returning things to their proper places.

"How are you doing?" he asked when she joined him in the kitchen.

"Okay." The word sounded flat. "They took my DVD player and a few pieces of jewelry. Nothing of any real value." She twisted the simple engagement ring and wedding band she still wore on her ring finger.

No. They'd taken more. They'd taken her sense of security. He'd seen the same haunted look on too many civilian faces in Iraq where people were scared of al-Qaeda, scared of insurgents, and scared of the US troops there to help them. The intruders may have even taken her husband's life. What if it had been the same men? What would they have done to her if she'd been here? His blood pounded in his temples at the scenarios he envisioned.

If he'd come down here when the alarm went off, he might have caught them rather than let them get away before the police arrived. Even if they had been armed, so was he, and he would have had the element of surprise. But he didn't have a way to restrain them. And as much as he wouldn't mind putting a bullet in them, there were laws. Shooting someone in her house could land him in jail. Get him kicked out of the Army. Only now, Stephanie's posture and darting eyes made him wish to hell he'd broken his promise and disobeyed her orders. That wasn't the only order he regretted following. But he couldn't go back in time to tell his teenage self to stand up to Nik's selfish request.

"Let's get out of here for a bit. I'll drop you back off at the condo, then hit the store to get what I need to reinforce the doors and alarm them and the windows." It might help restore a bit of her peace of mind to walk into the house without it looking like it'd been robbed.

"Good idea. I need to pick up Alexis so your parents can get on the road. Are you sure you—"

"Yes. I'm staying here. With you. I didn't say anything to my parents, but it takes a while to decompress after a deployment. Large crowds still put me on edge. I was going to appease them, but it's better I don't go. If I did, I'd be distracted finding emergency exits and evaluating everyone as a potential threat."

"Beyond who might say they object to the wedding?" She cracked a smile—her first of the day.

It shouldn't be that way. She had a beautiful smile. The

kind that made you smile back whether you wanted to or not. The kind that made the world brighter. The kind he could bask in every day and never tire of seeing. Already, he struggled with the thought of deserting her after his week of leave was up. Damn. It'd taken years to move past his infatuation with Stephanie. Or had he?

How long was a widow expected to wait before dating? Probably at least a year. Maybe less if she was young and hadn't been married long. Stephanie still wore her wedding rings, though. That might be a sign she wasn't ready. Why was he even torturing himself with imagining them together? In a few days he'd go back to Fort Campbell, six and a half hours away. It wasn't exactly practical—not that love had to be practical—but he was getting ahead of himself. He needed to focus on the situation at hand and not confuse her appreciation with romantic interest.

RAY BAGGED the last of the shrubbery clippings and hauled them to the curb. From there, he surveyed the front of Stephanie's house. With the bushes cut back, it'd be hard for anyone to hide there now. They hadn't heard back from the detective yet, but they hoped the video would lead to a break in the case.

It hadn't taken long to reinforce both doors into the house and show Stephanie how to install the peel-and-stick window alarms. They weren't tied to a security system that would alert the police, but those suckers were crazy-ass loud enough to wake Stephanie and the neighbors and scare off any normal person.

After putting the trimmers back in the storage shed, he did a last walk around the yard before heading in. He paused outside the back door, his hand on the knob. Inside, Stephanie bent over, peering into the open fridge. Even though he shouldn't be staring at her backside, he couldn't tear his gaze away from her enticing curves. He'd never been attracted to a twiggy figure, and Stephanie had ample curves in all the right places.

He already needed a shower from the yard work, but the way his dick stirred to attention whenever he imagined touching her, he'd better make it a long, cold one. A year-long deployment tended to make a guy pretty damn desperate, but this was Stephanie. She deserved better than being used because he'd been deprived of sex for so long—even if she had been deprived almost as long. No. He shouldn't justify it that way.

She straightened when he entered the kitchen.

"They didn't steal stuff out of the fridge, did they?"

"No. I was trying to scrounge up something to fix you for dinner."

"No need. I'm taking you out for dinner."

"You don't need to do that."

"I want to. In Iraq, I ate MREs once a day and chicken about five times a week. I'm overdue for a nice dinner, with a good steak—real beef—and I want to enjoy it conversing with a beautiful wom—friend—instead of listening for incoming mortars. When was the last time you had a night out?"

"It's been a while," she admitted. "Didn't you get a chance to take your girlfriend out before coming here?" She sounded nonchalant but her gaze flickered down and back.

Was she digging for his relationship status? "Uh, no girlfriend. I was, uh, seeing someone casually before I deployed, but it ended before I left."

"I can't believe she broke up with you because you were going to deploy."

That was hardly the case. In fact, Julia had suggested they get engaged, even dropped hints about getting married before he left. "It wasn't her. When I thought about the future, I couldn't see us together. It wouldn't be right to lead her on, so I ended things."

"Oh." Stephanie's indignant expression faded. "I see. That probably wasn't easy, but it sounds like it was the right thing to do."

It would have been nice to have someone special to talk to and look forward to his coming home, but Julia was clingy and insecure. Not ideal qualities for a military spouse. Deploying had given him an easy out since he sucked at ending relationships.

"I can't guarantee it'll be a fine dining experience with a toddler."

"I'm willing to run the risk. And I'd rather not be here after dark anyway. Why don't you change and pack whatever you need for the weekend, then we'll go down to Mom and Dad's condo, and I'll shower up."

"I've already packed more clothes. Give me a minute to change." She moved toward the high chair where Alexis ate cubes of cheese and ham.

"I'll watch her," he offered.

She stopped short and gave him a slight smile. "Thanks."

He didn't know what that smile was all about, but as long as he was on the receiving end, he didn't care.

He managed to entertain the toddler for the few minutes it took Stephanie to change. "Wow. You, uh, look fabulous," he told her when she came back wearing a green sundress with small white and yellow flowers on it. The

vibrant colors made the blue of her eyes pop and comple-
mented her blonde hair.

Her cheeks flushed to an attractive pink. "Too much? I
haven't had a reason to dress up lately."

"Not too much." That she'd put on makeup and a dress
that highlighted her figure sent his mind into overdrive. Had
she done that for him or herself? Not that it mattered. He
picked up the suitcase and bag of toys for Alexis.

Before opening the door, he peered out the front
window. Nothing looked suspicious, but he'd been gone a
long time and couldn't ID all the neighbors and their
vehicles.

"Let's go out the back." He hated the look of fear that
flashed across her face, but better to play it safe. Iraq taught
him to never, ever, let your guard down.

FIVE

While Ray showered, Stephanie entertained Alexis by rolling a ball back and forth on the wooden floor. Had she gone overboard in picking the dress and touching up her makeup? This wasn't a date, but Ray's appreciative gaze had her all aflutter. No harm in looking nice and indulging in a little fantasy.

Alexis captured the ball. Her adorable laughter echoed in the Lundgrens' nearly empty house. She pushed the ball back, managing to get it within Stephanie's reach. Alexis clapped her hands at her success, making Stephanie long for the sweet innocence of a child. Recent events had shattered any last vestiges of returning to those blissful days.

The ball rolled to Alexis's left, and she spun to grab for it. Losing her balance, she toppled forward. Stephanie winced at the thud of Alexis's head striking the floor. The wailing started before Stephanie could scoop her into her arms.

"Let me see, sweet baby." Stephanie brushed back the blonde curls and pressed a light kiss to the red welt over Alexis's left eye.

Tears rolled down her cheeks, and her nose ran as the bawling continued. Heavy footsteps approached behind them.

"What happened? Are you okay?" Ray demanded. His wide-eyed gaze darted around. Water droplets glistened on his chiseled face, his closely cropped blond hair, his bare chest, and muscular arms. His hand clutched the ends of the towel wrapped around his hips.

It took a second to tear her gaze from his barely covered body to answer him. "She fell and bumped her head. No blood, but she'll have a bump and bruise."

Alexis's sobs muffled when Stephanie cradled her to her chest and rubbed her back.

Ray's chest expanded as he drew in a deep breath, then slowly exhaled. She'd seen him shirtless plenty of times when he'd been a teen playing basketball with Nik and their friends, but this grown-up, bulked-up, toned-muscle version fanned the embers of attraction she'd always secretly harbored into full-on desire.

"I heard her scream, and I thought ..." He swallowed and stroked the back of Alexis's head, but his gaze locked on Stephanie with a longing expression that added fuel to the emotions blazing through her. "Why don't you get some ice while I get dressed?"

He didn't move; she didn't want to either. Alexis snuffled against her shoulder, prompting her to break the connection.

In the kitchen, she used one of the old dish towels left for cleaning to wrap up some ice cubes. The only furniture left in the house seemed to be in Ray's old bedroom, where she couldn't go, so she settled onto the floor and tried to apply the compress to Alexis's bump. Her daughter wasn't having any part of it. She squirmed and pushed at Stephanie's hands.

"It's to make your boo-boo better, sweetie."

"Boo-boo bunny," Alexis whined.

"I don't have it. It's at home."

"Want boo-boo bunny," she demanded in typical toddler fashion.

"Not this time." She got the ice pack on the knot for about thirty seconds. Not long enough to do much good. Ray would be out in a minute. After all his precautions, she was smart enough not to disappear on him to go over to her house where strangers had broken in, possibly to do her harm. Nope. She'd prefer to deal with the non-life-threatening contusion without the beloved bunny. She put the iced cloth to her forehead. "Mommy's turn."

"Mommy boo-boo?" Alexis put her hand over Stephanie's to help hold it.

"Mommy's all better," Stephanie proclaimed before Alexis lost interest. "Alexis's boo-boo." This time she iced the red spot about a minute before Ray appeared wearing dress slacks, a crisp, white button-down, and tie.

"Wow. I'm not the only one dressed up."

He shrugged. "I brought clothes for the rehearsal dinner and wedding. Figured I should look worthy of my beautiful dinner companions. How's her head?" He squatted to get closer to their level, frowning at the welt.

"Kids are resilient. It doesn't seem to be hurting now. We can still go out."

"Come on." He swooped up Alexis and extended a hand to Stephanie, pulling her up from the floor more gracefully than scrambling up on her own in the dress.

SIX

"Party of three," Ray said to the restaurant's hostess.

Her gaze roved over them before it shifted to the seating chart on the stand in front of her. "Give me a minute." She left them there, wove through the tables, and ducked into the back, reappearing a minute later with a high chair. She placed the chair at a table near the back, away from most of the other diners.

He scanned the dining room. Not a child in sight. They likely didn't have a kid's menu either. Okay, probably not the best choice of restaurants to bring a toddler on a busy Friday night, but they were here now.

The hostess had barely seated them before the server came over and set waters and a basket of bread on the table. "I'm Rebecca, and I'll be your server. Are you two celebrating anything special tonight?" Her gaze skimmed over Alexis.

"He just got back from a deployment to Iraq," Stephanie said.

"Thank you for your service." Rebecca gave him an

appreciative smile. "My cousin's in the Marines. He's in Fallujah right now. What branch?"

"Army. I was outside of Kirkuk for most of the year."

"A year? Wow. I can see why you want to be with both your wife *and* daughter after being away that long."

"Oh, we're not together that way. We're just old friends," Stephanie quickly corrected her.

"Sorry. I thought ..." Rebecca's gaze dropped to the wedding band on Stephanie's left hand.

Just old friends? Damn. After the past day, that hurt. He might have to accept that Stephanie wasn't ready to move on. Maybe he'd been misreading or imagining that there could be something more between them now. To hell with it. "I wanted to date her when I was in high school, except her brother wouldn't let me. But now—"

"What?" Stephanie exclaimed, shock clear on her face.

The server laughed. "I have an overprotective brother, too."

"You did?" Stephanie ignored the server. "And Nik ...? Did he really ...?" She slumped against the back of the chair, and her lips remained parted as she stared at him.

"Can I bring you wine or a cocktail while you look over the menu?" Rebecca broke the silence settling between them.

"Not yet. Give us a couple of minutes," Ray said, his heart beating harder and faster in his chest.

"When did Nik say that?" Stephanie asked once their server moved out of earshot.

"About a week after you came home from college."

"You mean right after you and I met?" Still looking stunned, she tore off a piece of bread and gave it to Alexis.

"Yeah." He'd seen pictures of her in the Laaksos' house, but meeting her had resulted in instant attraction. "I mentioned asking you to Laura Beaty's New Year's Eve party." He'd said sister, and Nik had presumed he meant Anni—who'd been less than discreet about her schoolgirl crush on Ray back then. When Ray clarified he meant Stephanie, Nik flipped out. "He said it would be a problem, especially if things didn't work out. If it'd been anyone else, I would have told him to"—he stopped before dropping the f-bomb in front of Alexis—"go screw himself. But your brother was the first friend I made when I moved here."

"Because you were the same age and we lived two doors down."

"True. Except he was my *best* friend by then. With me being in high school and you being a college student home for the holidays ... Nik said his sisters were off-limits—and I followed orders." Except she hadn't gone back to college the next semester and he kept falling harder and harder for her.

"So, instead, you and Nik took the Ferguson twins to that party?"

"That was Nik's idea."

"Because he heard Wendy put out."

His burst of laughter drew a few glances from other diners. Stephanie's ability to read people and shoot it straight were qualities that drew him to her, and she'd nailed her brother's motivation. No point in denying it, but he didn't want her thinking he'd had the same intentions. "She was the wild twin, that's for sure. Nik needed a wingman since Wendy and Emily were a package deal."

"They didn't last long, but you dated Emily for like six months."

She remembered that? "No. She *thought* we were dating for about that long. We went on like three double dates with Nik and Wendy and one solo date."

"Really?" She grilled him with a stare so skeptical he squirmed under her scrutiny.

"Really!" he swore to her. "She was a cheerleader, so she was at all the basketball games. The team and the cheerleading squad usually got pizza and hung out at after games. That didn't count as dates. I didn't know how to get her to realize she wasn't my girlfriend. She wasn't the sharpest tool in the shed."

An amused half-laugh escaped Stephanie. "Neither was Wendy. How Nik put up with her for those few weeks, I'll never know."

"I prefer women who, like you, are beautiful and intelligent and self-sufficient."

She dipped her head. "Nik used to make a point to tell me you weren't into book nerds like me, so I ... Well, all that's in the past. We moved on. I didn't mean to make things awkward." She picked up the wine list and studied it like her life depended on it.

He'd obeyed Nik's orders, but then they grew up and went their separate ways. There wasn't anything stopping him from taking this relationship beyond the friend zone now. He wasn't going to let this opportunity get blown to hell. "Is it? In the past?" He set the wine list down and waited for her to look at him. "Because a lot of times when you're moving, you aren't going in a straight line. You circle back to where you started. Then you can—"

"Are you ready to order drinks now?"

Stephanie's attention jerked to Rebecca, who'd emerged to interrupt him at the worst possible moment. "I'll, um, have a glass of zinfandel."

"I'll have the pinot noir," he threw out.

Rebecca didn't move. "Do you have any questions about the menu?"

Ray ground his teeth together and counted to three because ten would take too long. "How about I give you a signal when we're ready to order?"

"O—kay." She slowly backed away with a self-conscious smile, one he hoped meant she wouldn't interrupt again.

"As I was saying." What had he been saying? "I need to know if it is in the past. I'll still be here to protect you, but I need to adjust my expectations about what's going on here. Between us. Are we just friends? Because I'd like for this to be a date."

Stephanie swallowed, her gaze darting around. "Do you often bring a toddler on dates?"

Was she stalling, or worse, dodging? He remained steadfast. "This is my first time. I hope it won't be the last."

"You're only here for a few days. Then you'll be back in Kentucky."

"Kentucky isn't Italy or Seattle. It's drivable for a weekend."

Stephanie's scrunched expression when she tilted her head toward Alexis happily chewing on the bread made him envision spending seven hours on the road with a toddler.

"*I* can make the drive. We can talk and video chat. How about instead of looking for reasons not to, we look for reasons to give us a shot? One step at a time. Then, if we like where things are going, we put in the effort to take things to the next level." He waited, keeping his eyes locked on hers for what felt like minutes.

The corners of her mouth turned up in a mischievous grin. "Would we have to keep it secret from my brother?"

"That's up to you." He was done taking orders from Nik. He wished he never had.

"There's no reason for him to have a say in what

happens in our lives. He's been kind of a selfish ass for lying to me so he wouldn't risk losing you as a friend."

"If he has a problem with us and he wants to act like a jerk, fine. I don't need him."

"Yes—this is a date. To hell with what Nik thinks."

The smile on her face was more than contagious, and the emotions rushing through his body went beyond sexual attraction. He hadn't felt this way about a woman in—ever. "All right then. This is officially a date. I'm paying, and you lovely ladies can order whatever you want. But, at the end of the night, I am hoping for a kiss." He drew the words out while holding her gaze.

Alexis covered her mouth with her hand, made a kissing sound, and blew the kiss toward Stephanie. "Mm-ma."

That wasn't exactly what he had in mind, but the toddler's simple, sweet gesture added to the natural high he was riding at the moment.

He signaled Rebecca to bring their wine and take their order. This called for a bit of a celebration.

ONCE THE TRUTH had come out and Ray pressed her, it'd taken Stephanie a minute to decide if she was ready for this. The last few months, she barely had time to think about dating, much less meet anyone, because of the grind of being responsible for herself and her daughter. But loneliness had settled in, and she wanted companionship. Someone to talk with. Make decisions with. She didn't want to risk losing Ray as a friend, but she didn't want to pass up the opportunity to see if they could be more. He was single. She was—again. And all the old feelings were back. It might not go anywhere, but what did she have to lose? Not more than she'd already lost.

After she'd agreed this was a date, the mood shifted. The awkwardness dissipated, and the evening had been fun, relaxed, and even romantic, despite having Alexis make it a party of three. A box of baby wipes wouldn't take the smile off Stephanie's face as they headed out of the restaurant after dinner. She was totally going to kick her brother's ass the next time she saw him, though she might need Ray to hold him down for her to do it.

"Wait here a minute." Ray stopped her before opening the heavy wooden doors.

For the past hour, their conversation had taken her mind off everything else. Her full stomach clenched, and that peace vanished as he scanned the parking lot. She hugged Alexis closer to her chest.

Ray turned back with what should have been a reassuring smile and motioned for her to come. In a few days, he wouldn't be here to make her feel safe. Then what?

He remained at her side while she climbed in to buckle Alexis into the car seat. Did he feel like he needed to stand on guard duty? Never in her life had she been a risk-taker, and she couldn't go on like this.

She wiggled out of the tight space to find him staring at her.

"Is it okay to kiss you in front of Alexis, or would you prefer to wait?"

Her insides went all melty that it occurred to him to ask. "At this age, I don't think it would scar her for life if she saw me kiss someone." Good Lord, the smile he gave her made her insides quiver. She leaned slightly toward him and hoped she didn't appear desperate. If he didn't kiss her soon, she wouldn't be liable for what she might do. "I think we've waited long enough."

"Agreed." His deep voice dropped even lower, as did his face.

Her face tilted up, and her eyes closed before their lips met.

Ray tasted like a hint of wine, but more like the mint he'd grabbed on the way out. He smelled fresh and clean from the shower, and the softness of his freshly shaven skin countered the hard muscles of his arms beneath her hands.

She'd crushed on him for well over a year, even when he'd dated Emily, and she'd imagined kissing him dozens, if not hundreds, of times. After he left for college, it'd still taken her a while to get over her infatuation. She'd told herself that reality couldn't possibly live up to her fantasies.

But with his hands on her hips and their bodies close, she could say with absolute certainty that, in this case, reality trumped fantasy. His lips moved gently against hers in a teasing manner that made her want more. She didn't care that they were making out in a public parking lot like a pair of teenagers. Some things were worth waiting for.

DRIVING BACK TO RAY'S PARENTS' condo, they held hands and reminisced about their families and mutual friends. For the most part, anchoring her thoughts to the past batted away the recurring worries about the two fake detectives, except talking about her parents brought her back to the dilemma of her future. Hers and Alexis's. It was too soon to let her feelings for Ray play a part in her decision. Things might not even go anywhere, especially since he had to return to his base in a couple of days.

Alexis nodded off on the drive, but not soundly enough to stay asleep once they got home. Stephanie tried not to rush as she changed her for bed and read a book. She closed the book and kissed Alexis on the top of her head. "Time to go night-night." After the nap in the car, she gave it about a sixty–forty chance of Alexis going back to sleep. With Ray waiting to pick up where they'd left off, she hoped the odds were in her favor.

Her daughter's wide-eyed gaze followed her as Stephanie climbed off the bed and turned off the light. "I love you. See you in the morning." Hopefully, that little stay-in-bed warning would suffice.

Nothing else was going right in her life the past few months, so she closed the door expecting to hear a cry. Nothing. She'd count that as one small miracle.

Before joining Ray, she ducked into the guest bathroom to freshen up. The effect of those earlier kisses lingered, making her want more. Her heart beat hard enough to make her feel it, and her arms trembled.

While she brushed her teeth, her mind went on a dizzying journey. Grief, work, and Alexis gave her little time or energy to think about sex. Ray had been deployed for a year and hadn't come home to a girlfriend. Was it possible it'd been even longer for him? A well-meaning friend had given her an adult toy shortly after Sam's death. She'd used it a few times, but it certainly wasn't the same as being with a living, breathing man with his own needs.

How fast would this go? Where would they ...? Damn. She'd put Alexis to bed in the guest room without thinking it through. There were only two bedrooms in the condo. That left the master. Would she be able to look his parents in the eye if they had sex in their bed? She felt like a high school girl about to lose her virginity while the parents were away.

Instead of trying to plot this out, she needed to chill. Let Ray take the lead. He might have a plan. That was more his style and personality anyway. She dug through her makeup bag and applied a fresh coat of lip gloss, with the hope it'd be kissed off soon.

She ran a brush through her hair, and her shoulders sank when Ray's voice carried to her. *Great.* Alexis must be up and looking for her. Well, that would give them more time to transition to the romance part of tonight's date. Alexis had only a short nap this afternoon; she would crash for the night soon.

With the pressure scaled back, she opened the bathroom door and found the guest room door still closed. As she neared the kitchen, she made out that Ray's tone was deeper than the timbre he'd used to speak to Alexis all day.

"Here she is." Ray held out her phone to her. "It's Detective Boothe."

She'd given up hearing from him today. Her emotions spun into a whirlwind when she took the phone. "Hi." Her voice cracked.

"Sorry to call so late. I got caught up in another case this afternoon and just got back to the precinct. I've got mug shots I'd like you and Sergeant Lundgren to look at. The sooner we ID the men who broke into your house, the better chance we have of picking them up. I'd like to get their pictures out to the morning patrol. I can be there in twenty minutes."

She got the impression he wasn't asking permission as much as telling them he was coming. "We'll be here." She hung up and gave Ray an apologetic smile. Twenty minutes didn't give them time to finish anything. Better not to start.

They stared at each other until she broke the silence with a sigh.

"Glass of wine?" he offered.

"Better wait until after we do the ID."

"Good point. Come here." He held out his hand and jerked his head toward the terrace.

His hand clasped hers and lent her a bit of his strength as they stepped out into the warm night. The setting sun painted the sky in shades of pink, orange, and gold that reflected off the surface of the lake. She watched two people on wave runners race over the open water. Further out, several pontoon boats motored slowly or bobbed on the water. She soaked in the tranquility.

"I see why your parents wanted to move out here."

"Me, too. Dad's already looking at boats. Mom loves the view. It's especially beautiful tonight." He delivered that line looking at her in a way that set her skin afire. "How long until Boothe will be here?"

"About twenty minutes."

"Not a lot of time, but we should use it wisely." He leaned closer as he said it, slowly invading her space.

She turned her face up, inviting further invasion—of her space, her mouth, her anything he wanted. All she could think about was how good it felt. To be kissed. To be held. To not be alone.

When Boothe knocked, Ray gave her a last reassuring squeeze, then strode to the front door. He returned to the living room with the disheveled detective on his heels. One side of his shirt was untucked, and the knot of his loosened tie hit below the second button. His buzzed hair stood at attention. He pushed his glasses up with his index finger only to have them slide back down his nose.

"Would you like some water or coffee?" Stephanie asked.

"Just water."

Ray led them to the kitchen. While Stephanie filled a glass, the detective pulled a stack of pictures from his coat pocket. He shrugged out of the jacket, then dropped it over the back of a chair. He separated the pictures into two piles and handed the thicker stack to Ray.

"See if any of these look familiar. We didn't find a good match for the redhead claiming to be Farmer. Maybe we'll get lucky." He motioned for Stephanie to sit, then placed the pictures in front of her.

She sifted through the few mug shots of redheaded men. Not one looked remotely like the quiet, fake detective with the intimidating scowl. "Definitely none of these." She handed the pictures to Ray, and he traded stacks with her.

She studied each thoroughly, hoping the next one would be one of the men who'd come to her house. Her hopes hurtled out the window when she reached the last picture. She sighed and handed the pile back. "He's not in here."

"Are you sure?" He pulled out two of the pictures. "Did you look closely at these?"

Ray moved his chair closer and looked at them, too. "He didn't have a scar."

She handed back that picture before staring at the other again.

"Try to imagine him clean-shaven, with shorter hair, wearing a dress shirt and tie."

Doubt pecked at her brain like a chicken at feed. "I'm sure. His eyes were brown, not blue."

"She's right," Ray agreed.

"All right. They may not be locals like I'd hoped. We'll have to run the screen captures through the national database, which will take longer." Boothe gathered the pictures. "Since you mentioned to Mr. Floyd giving police a description, these guys might lie low. Don't know they'd go so far as to leave town. Have you made a decision about going back to try and get information on the delivery carrier he uses?"

"I've been thinking it through." All afternoon. She'd probably run through a dozen scenarios. Right now, it didn't look like she had much choice.

"You go when they're closed. It won't be a big deal." Boothe made it sound simple.

"After Sam was killed, Gary upgraded the security system." Now, she'd bet money the old system *not* working that night was a lie, and it was tampered with later. The sons of bitches. "The new system takes a picture anytime the front door is opened. If anything is out of place—"

"He looks at the tape and knows you were there." The detective frowned.

"The real problem is that he keeps the files in a locked cabinet in his office—which he also keeps locked." The reason for that made more sense now.

"If I were to help you break in, we couldn't use anything to get a warrant, and any evidence wouldn't stand up in court. That's a no-go."

"I can take care of the locks." Confident bravado came through in Ray's tone.

"*You* need to stay out of this. This isn't Iraq. Leave it to the proper authorities."

"But you're—"

"That's an order." He cut Ray off and fixed his attention solely on her. "Since we can't go in during off-hours, we have some time. Maybe we'll get a break and find them. Give it some more thought." Boothe got to his feet. "I'm out of the office for the weekend, but they'll keep me updated. If I hear anything, I'll let you know. I'll be sure to touch base on Sunday at the latest. Use caution if you go out."

Ray stood, too. "I'll walk you out."

The message that Ray wanted a private word with the detective came through clearly, and she wasn't going to fight him on that. She was the one who had to decide about the next step. At least she had time. Not much, but maybe it'd be enough to get clarity on things with Ray and the best way to keep her and Alexis safe.

AFTER STEPPING outside with Detective Boothe, Ray closed the door behind them.

"I'm not on board with sending her back there and putting her in danger. Let me go. I can pose as a customer and—"

"What did I tell you? You need to leave this to us. The two who came to her house probably blame you being there for why they weren't able to nab her. You're what, six-five?"

"A little over six-four. Barefoot."

Boothe peered over the top of his glasses at him. "You're kind of memorable. You show up there, and you blow everything."

"Then do surveillance of the dealership."

"We don't have the manpower for that. And *you* are not doing it either."

That wasn't an option with having to report to post in a few days anyway. If he was late getting back, he could be confined, his pay could be docked, or worse, depending on how long he was AWOL. "What about putting up surveillance cameras?"

"If we get solid evidence, we can make that happen. That's why we need her to go. Get a name. Dates. Ultimately, it's Mrs. Anderson's choice. I can't make her go. But, if you talk her out of it, then whoever killed her husband may get away with it and"—he paused—"and we won't know if she remains a target. Give her a place to stay, watch over her, but leave solving the case to us." He drilled Ray with another stare.

No promises.

He didn't want Sam's killers getting away with it; however, protecting Stephanie and Alexis was his priority. Could he find a way to ensure their long-term safety when he had to leave in three days? How many more days could he take off? He wasn't about to leave Stephanie in this vulnerable position, but he couldn't risk going AWOL either. Ray headed back inside.

Stephanie's singsong voice told him that Alexis was up. He was right. In the kitchen, she sat on Stephanie's lap, sipping a cup of milk.

"She didn't go back to sleep?"

"I'm not sure. Could be some voices woke her." Stephanie met his eyes with a look of clear disappointment.

Damn, he should have realized that he and the detective were right outside her bedroom window.

Alexis muttered something he couldn't understand.

"I'm sorry, honey," Stephanie cooed, "*Dragon Tales* isn't on right now."

"I wan' *Dragon Tales.*"

This time he managed to decipher what she said.

"Sorry, baby, but it's only on in the morning." Stephanie gave him a doleful look. "It's her favorite show. I have a

DVD at home for her to watch. Maybe we can find something else that will entertain her until she's ready to fall back asleep."

The toddler's inquisitive eyes were alert while Stephanie could barely keep hers open. After getting little sleep last night, it looked like he and Stephanie would need to change their plans from what they had in mind.

In a few minutes, he'd gathered enough blankets and pillows to set up a makeshift bed on the floor in the living room. Stephanie gave Alexis blocks to play with, then she flipped through TV programs, finally settling on something on Animal Planet. Ray helped Alexis stack blocks while Stephanie stretched out on the blankets, her eyes quickly closing. She'd had one hell of a long and stressful day.

It didn't take long before Alexis was yawning. She finished her milk, then cuddled up next to her mom. The sight of the two stirred up Ray's protective nature. He watched them sleep for a few minutes before turning off the television and settling down beside them.

SEVEN

B ecause of a spring shower, they spent a few hours in the morning unpacking boxes at the condo. Once the sun came out, they hit the park. Over an hour on the playground, a picnic lunch, then feeding bread to the ducks and geese had been the near-perfect kind of day that Stephanie had envisioned spending with Alexis and Sam. After having those dreams stolen from her, she wasn't going to let a nap schedule rule her day. But the stop at the grocery store proved to be too much.

Stephanie lifted a fussy Alexis out of the shopping cart. "I'm sorry. I knew we were pushing the limits," she said to Ray.

Would he drop his bodyguard role long enough to take Alexis out to the car and let her finish the grocery shopping on her own? She didn't want to make them go back out again. She needed to grab a few staples for Alexis and get what she wanted to cook for Ray tonight.

"Here." Ray reached out to take Alexis from her.

It was amazing how, in a day and a half, Ray had gone from being clueless on how to hold a toddler to *offering* to take Alexis. Even more surprising, Alexis went to him without hesitation. He held her easily with one arm, and within seconds her head rested against his shoulder. Not a bad place to be.

When Stephanie woke in the middle of the night to find Ray also asleep on the floor, she couldn't bring herself to leave him there alone or wake him, even though he deserved to sleep in a comfortable bed. Maybe it was the months of being alone, but his nearness helped ease her loneliness.

In a few days, he would have to leave. Was a long-distance relationship really doable? Or was it her old, unrequited crush making her hope this was real? Fear could also be playing a role in her feelings, and his. Once he believed her safe, and he was back home, would she be out of his thoughts? She watched Ray swaying in place while the meat department clerk wrapped the salmon steaks in paper. Despite the risk of getting her heart shattered again, she melted at the sight of Alexis asleep on his shoulder.

Ray wandered off for a minute, returning to slip a box in the cart. When she tossed in a bag of coffee, she caught a glimpse of the condoms. Not the large box, but not the three-pack either. A volcano erupted inside her, based on the heat radiating through her and settling between her legs. She didn't dare make eye contact for fear the lustful thoughts going through her head would be written all over her face.

She breezed down the aisles, getting the rest of the groceries and paying before Ray could whip out his wallet.

Alexis barely stirred when Stephanie wrangled her out of the car seat back at the condo. When Stephanie laid her on the guest bed, she stuck her thumb in her mouth, and her eyes closed.

"How long will she sleep?" Ray asked when Stephanie

returned to find him putting away groceries in the kitchen. She didn't see the box of condoms anywhere.

"Probably around two hours."

"I'll hold off on putting up the bookshelves, so the pounding doesn't wake her."

"She might sleep through it."

"I'd rather not risk it. I'm sure we can think of something else to do that won't wake her."

His intense gaze traveled from her eyes to her mouth to her chest, then lower, before returning to her face. It clearly conveyed his meaning about *playing* house—not setting up his parents' home. She took a step closer to let him know what she thought of that plan but made him close the remaining distance.

His hand slid to the small of her back, and his tender touch made her shiver in a delicious way. Staring into her eyes, he took his time. Finally, slowly, he dipped his head, and she tilted her face in invitation. Still, he made her wait, teasing her with his nearness until she rose on her tiptoes and brushed her lips to his.

His fingers splayed on her lower back, while his right hand anchored to the wall so that his body held her in place. The intensity of his kiss increased. His lips parted, and his tongue glided over her lips. Her mouth opened to welcome his exploration.

His hand left the wall and slid over her hair to the back of her head. He inched his left hand lower to cup her bottom, pulling her body against his and leaving no doubt of his aroused state, which sent another flow of desire raging through her. It set off a blaze beyond her control. Not that she wanted to control it.

His mouth left hers when he lifted her off her feet. He easily held her, and she wrapped her legs around his waist like something out of a steamy scene in a movie. There was something incredibly arousing about being pinned against the wall and being taller than Ray for once.

He shifted her even higher. His mouth trailed over her neck with hot, passion-infused kisses. She pressed her head back to give him full access to her sensitive throat, simultaneously jutting her hips into him. She cradled his head, refusing to let him stop, even though she wanted to slide lower and make contact with something as hard as the muscled abdomen pressing intimately against her and making her crazy with need.

His low growl rumbled against her chest and amped her lust up another notch, only his mouth left her skin, prompting her to release a breathy protest. Ray gave a half chuckle, half grunt as he shifted his weight. "Oh, we're not done. We're just getting started. I promise."

She liked the sound of that promise. If Detective Boothe called and interrupted them again, she might be the one guilty of murder.

Supporting her with one arm, Ray turned them and pulled a chair from the kitchen table, then lowered himself onto it with her straddling his lap. His fingers lazily traced up her sides. Her breasts had stayed full even after pregnancy. Still, his sizable hands easily covered and caressed them with the perfect amount of pressure.

She kneaded his strong shoulders and stroked his broad back as they kissed. Soon his warm hands slid under her shirt, eliminating one layer of the clothing between them. Her nipples tingled under his touch. "Take it off," she whispered between kisses.

He gripped the hem of her top and eased the shirt up her body, his fingers connecting with her skin at every opportunity before he slipped the shirt over her head. His gaze roved over her, and he ran his hands along her lower back, letting his fingertips brush under the waistband of her shorts. When his touch lingered on the hooks of her bra, she reached up to unfasten it. Seconds later, he peeled the fabric away. He stared, swallowing visibly. Ray was the first man to see her bare breasts since Sam. But she wanted more than him seeing them.

Shamelessly, she leaned into his hands, relishing how his touch made her feel more alive, more complete than she'd felt in months. She'd missed this more than she'd realized. Missed it enough to delight in the scandalous sensation of being exposed to him in broad daylight. They both wanted this. To hell with what anyone else would think.

She grabbed hold of Ray's T-shirt and yanked it up. He compliantly raised his arms. After he wrangled his shirt off, he pulled her against his chest, giving her the skin-on-skin contact she craved. Their kisses were needy and greedy—as if neither could get enough of the other after years of suppressing their attraction.

She had no idea how much time had passed before the kissing and fondling and grinding had her desperate for more. Maybe Ray sensed it because he guided her off his lap. Once she stood in front of him, his hot breath heated her flesh as his lips grazed her belly. A hungry murmur escaped her when his fingers unbuttoned her shorts. The faint sound of the zipper's teeth separating as he tugged the pull down slowly made her more eager for the next step.

He lowered the rough denim shorts to her thighs, then ran his hands up her calves, all the way to her hips. "You're so beautiful." His low voice whispered the words reverently, despite her abdomen pouching out in a way it hadn't pre-pregnancy and the faded stretch marks lining her sides.

When he pushed to his feet, she couldn't ignore the

ample bulge in his shorts, but he showed no sign of self-consciousness. Instead, he took her hand and led her to the family room. He grabbed hold of the blanket she'd neatly folded up that morning and spread it on the floor over the thick pile rug, then dropped the pillows to the floor.

After all these years, all her fantasies, this was really happening. She and Ray Lundgren were going to make love. Emboldened, she hooked her thumb in the waistband of her panties.

"Not yet." He stopped her. "I'm gonna want to do that."

Oh, good Lord. On the brink of melting into a pool of molten desire, she sank to the floor before her knees gave out. He didn't immediately join her, and she waited in impatient anticipation as he repositioned himself so he could wrangle off his gym shorts after discreetly palming a condom.

He watched her while he removed his boxers. Holy cow. His erection snapped to attention and eliminated any question of whether he was well-proportioned all over.

The briefest flicker of hesitation crossed his face before she smiled at him, and he dropped to his knees between her legs. Supporting his weight on both hands, he lowered his head to kiss her right breast, drawing her into his mouth and swirling his tongue over her sensitive nipple. He mimicked his ministrations on her left breast before pressing kisses to her ribcage, then her belly. The weight of his body on hers made her writhe needily against him. His mouth covered her belly button, his tongue dipping in to tease her there. Then he went lower, kissing and nipping at her inner thigh.

When his tongue skimmed higher, her body jolted, and her hand flew down to push his face away.

He jerked his head and stared at her in surprise. Several seconds passed. Fear froze her lungs, and now it was self-consciousness that sent the uncomfortable heat racing through her. "You okay? Did I ...?"

"No. It's ..." Damn, she was going to disappoint him with her naiveté and limited sexual experience.

"Have you never had a guy go down on you?"

She shook her head. Sam was the only man she'd made love to. It'd been nice, but it hadn't been anything wild or adventurous.

"It's been a long time for me, and I want to make sure you aren't disappointed in any way," he said with humble sincerity.

That did sound good, and it had been a very long time, but ...

"Trust me. I'm not going to hurt you." He waited.

She gave a nod of acquiescence and settled onto her back, willing her body to relax as Ray started kissing her left hip above her pelvis. His tongue trailed a path lower, still in the safety zone, though he wove his fingers through the curls of hair between her legs. One thick finger stroked and dipped inside her, spreading her moisture while his thumb teased her clit, eliciting delicate moans as she neared her peak.

He transitioned smoothly, and when his mouth took the place of his hand, she didn't flinch. Ray looped his arm under her hamstrings, spreading her legs to open her more fully. Her trepidation faded, and her hips rose off the floor to encourage his tongue's deeper exploration. Millions of nerves tingled, and her calf muscles tightened in anticipation as she hovered on the brink. Her body bucked as the orgasm crested and broke in waves so intense she had to jostle his head away due to the overwhelming sensations that made her raw to the touch.

She opened her eyes when Ray worked his way up her trembling body, pressing random kisses along the way.

"That's what I wanted to do for you," he said in a tone that made her want more.

Saying *thank you* didn't seem adequate after the gift he had given her, both in terms of pleasure and education. There was another way she could thank him.

She aimed her best sultry smile at him. "Your turn."

———

"TELL me again why you listened to my brother." Sated desire laced Stephanie's voice as she tickled a pattern over Ray's chest with her index finger.

"Because I was stupid." His fingers threaded into her hair in a possessive claim. Her body melded into his like a perfect fit. Why the hell had he obeyed Nik's request not to date his sister? It's not like that had been an actual order he had to follow. And sometimes orders sucked or were just plain wrong. Following them blindly didn't make you a good soldier. If he'd followed his gut then, he and Stephanie might have dated. Who knows, even married. At least they were finally getting a chance. They had a lot of lost time to make up for.

"I'd never use the word 'stupid' to describe you."

His ego swelled at her continued confidence in him. He pulled her closer and kissed the top of her head. "Guess being in JROTC taught me to follow orders." Especially if he wanted to become a leader.

"*You* were in JROTC. My brother wasn't. You didn't have to take orders from him."

"Maybe not. But it was my way of showing respect to my

best friend." He learned that lesson in high school when Peter, the Army JROTC battalion commander, had talked back to their math teacher again—disobeying the captain's orders to keep his big mouth shut. The captain didn't issue a second warning. He'd made Daniel Harter the new commander. No matter what Peter did after that, he'd never earned back the captain's respect. "If I had it to do over again, I'd totally disobey Nik's order." Ray positioned himself over Stephanie.

She grinned up at him. "Good. Because skilled leaders issue orders."

"I like the idea of giving orders. I can't guarantee they'll be good. They might be kind of naughty."

"Mmm," she murmured. "Really? Then I hope you're still good at taking them, because I might have to issue some, too."

Those might be a very different kind of orders than he was used to—but also ones he wouldn't mind taking.

EIGHT

Rather than keep up with the Bobcats basketball game on TV, Ray's attention was riveted on Alexis placing chunky wooden pieces in a puzzle.

Alexis picked up another piece and put it in the right slot.

"Very good. That's the sheep. What does it say?" Stephanie prompted.

Alexis's cute little mouth puckered up. "*Mooo!*"

"Sheep say *baa*," Stephanie corrected her. "Cows say *moo*." She pointed to the cow piece already in the puzzle. "Where is the horse?"

"*Moo*," Alexis said again.

Ray couldn't help but laugh. "She really likes the cow." Or at least the sound. "*Moo!*"

"All right, Sergeant Smarty-Pants, it's your turn." Stephanie pushed the puzzle in his direction.

"I think I can do that puzzle in about three seconds."

"You'll need a handicap." She pushed to her feet and disappeared into his parents' bedroom.

She emerged a few seconds later with his mom's sleep mask from the nightstand—the one he'd hinted at using when they'd fooled around again last night. His expression clearly gave away what popped into his mind based on the look she gave him. He shrugged.

"On the floor."

"That an order?" he teased.

She pointed. He slid off the couch to the floor. When she handed him the mask, he got even harder at the ideas it gave him.

"Put it on and *no* peeking."

Did she really have no idea of the way he could take everything she was saying? Or maybe the point was, she *did* know.

He listened while she moved things around on the floor in front of him, taking longer than it should have.

"No, honey, it's—Ray's turn."

Had she been about to refer to him in a different way? The hesitation before saying his name made him long to pull her into his lap. To make her promises.

"I'm not going to time you, but I'm not giving you hints either. You may begin." Stephanie sounded both matter-of-fact and amused.

He picked up the first piece his fingers touched. Though it filled Alexis's fist, the small shape was indiscernible in his calloused hand. It took him a few attempts trying to fit the piece in to realize she'd rotated the puzzle. He spun it one hundred eighty degrees. The second piece was the roundish shape of the pig or sheep. He maneuvered it into place. She had barely slowed him down despite the blindfold. The third only took two seconds. Boom! He picked up another piece and—nope. He turned it. When it still didn't fit, he slid it to the other opening. What the ...? He would not take off the blindfold and forfeit. *Think!*

He set the piece aside, felt around, and came up with another. Voilà! It settled in easily. He expanded his reach and found two more pieces for the remaining slot. The little trickster.

When Stephanie and Alexis clapped after he finished the puzzle, he took that as permission to remove the blindfold. "Sneaky," he said in response to Stephanie's coy smile.

"Gotta be able to think outside the box. Besides, kids sometimes dump all the puzzles or toys on the floor to test you." She screwed up her face looking at Alexis.

Even that goofy face made him fall more in love with her. If only she knew how far outside the box she already had him thinking.

He might not know much about kids, but his comfort level had risen from about a two to probably a six out of ten. Not a bad learning curve for three days. And Alexis already had him willing to slay dragons for her. It wouldn't be fair for her to grow up without a father. With her golden blonde curls, deep blue eyes, and the dimple in her left cheek, she'd need someone to keep the boys in line. Preferably someone who knew how to handle an M4 rifle.

And Stephanie didn't deserve what had happened to Sam and how it upended her life and dreams. She knew she wanted to be a wife and mother. From what Nik had spilled to Ray, she'd gone to college and studied nursing at her parents' insistence that it would be a great career for her because of her caregiver tendencies. However, with her empathetic nature, seeing people in pain drained the life and joy out of her. After Stephanie told her parents she wasn't going back, they thought working a year or two in an "unskilled labor" job would change her perspective about needing a degree.

Ray admired that she had the self-awareness to know what she wanted and confidence and fortitude not to let others, including her parents, push her into life choices they made for her. He'd also bucked his parent's wishes when he dropped out of classes and enlisted.

Since he'd planned to make a career out of the military, why wait to get through another three and a half years of college to join the fight? With Operation Enduring Freedom and now Operation Iraqi Freedom raging, he knew he'd made the right decision. But he'd also sacrificed a lot.

Was it crazy to think about marriage already? Half his buddies in his platoon were married. McPherson had only dated Kiersten for three months before they married a few weeks before their unit deployed, knowing he had a wife back home had grounded and matured him. Kept him from taking unnecessary risks. And from what Ray had seen, the McPhersons stayed strong despite the year apart.

Then there'd been Ekwonu sweeping Amaka into his arms at their homecoming. The big guy crying stuck in Ray's mind. He'd proposed a week later and asked Ray to be his best man. For half a minute, Ray had second-guessed his decision to end things with Julia. But Julia wasn't what—or who—he wanted. He'd known it then, and he sure as hell knew it now. The last day and a half had shown him how compatible he and Stephanie were.

An image of the future, her as his wife, more children, was a vision that sat well with him. In light of everything going on in Stephanie's life, it was a reasonable thought. They didn't have to rush, but she and Alexis could come back to Fort Campbell with him where they'd be safe.

Where they could give this relationship a serious shot while Detective Boothe and the department worked on solving Sam's murder.

Stephanie already knew she couldn't go back to work, and he would be here to back her and make sure Boothe accepted that was not an option. Surely, the authorities could come up with a better plan than sending a young, untrained, widowed mother of a toddler in to do their investigative work.

NINE

"**D**inner was delicious. Thank you," Ray delivered a compliment to go with his empty plate.

"You're welcome. It's nice to cook something more elaborate than chicken fingers and macaroni and cheese."

"After a year of eating at the DFAC, the dining facility on base," he clarified, "and MREs, you're definitely spoiling me."

"It's the least I can do." She gathered plates and carried them to the sink so he wouldn't see her blush. Using her talents to take care of him made her feel useful and provided some payback for all he'd done for her and Alexis.

"I'll do KP since you cooked." He brought over his plate and the bowl with the leftover shrimp and pasta she fixed tonight and set them on the counter. From behind, he slipped an arm around her and pulled her body back against his. He nuzzled her hair out of the way to kiss along the side of her neck.

Help and fooling around in the kitchen. This was something she could get used to. Only Alexis didn't ignore them for long.

"All done. Wan' down, Mommy."

"Does Alexis want a cookie?"

"Cookie!"

She couldn't be the perfect mother all the time. Stephanie slipped from Ray's grasp to reach for the box of animal crackers. Giving Alexis three should buy them a minute or two.

They'd barely started kissing, and Ray hadn't even copped a feel before her phone started ringing.

Thanks to Ray, she had managed to block out thoughts of the fake detectives for hours at a time, but with one look at her caller ID, her fantasy world crumbled.

"Hello, Detective Boothe," she answered, the heavy weight returning.

"I wanted to give you an update," he said without preamble. "Is it okay if I stop by in about ten minutes?" His tone didn't give away anything, but could this be good news?

"That's fine. We're at the Lundgrens'." She clicked off and turned to Ray. "Detective Boothe's on his way over. Since I'm not sure how long this will take, I'll change Alexis if you don't mind cleaning up the kitchen."

"No problem."

Ray's composure didn't change; however, her mood switched to the dark side. She tried to focus on the positive as she changed Alexis into her pajamas. She'd just returned to the family room when the detective knocked. Ray headed to the door while she settled Alexis on the floor with her blocks.

Instead of his customary gray slacks, button-down shirt, and loosened tie, Detective Boothe looked undercover in his tan shorts, dock shoes, and an untucked light pink collared shirt.

"I wish I had better news." He took a seat in the chair across from the couch, his gaze lingering on Alexis for several seconds before he continued. "Even with the video, we haven't been able to ID the two men who broke into your house. We might still get a match, but these things take time, and it's the end of the weekend. Which leaves us with what to do about you going into work tomorrow."

"She can't go back there," Ray interrupted before Stephanie could open her mouth.

"This isn't your decision," she reminded him. "What would you need me to do?" She redirected her stare to the detective.

"But—" Ray started.

"I mean it." She silenced him with a stern, direct look. His jaw locked shut, but his glowering expression spoke loudly.

"Go into work. Act like it's a normal day." Boothe proceeded like Ray wasn't there. "When you have a chance, pull records to see who their carriers are—do not ask. Look for records of delivery dates, past and present, and take a picture or make copies. We can check the dates to see if there was a delivery around Sam's murder."

"So, I wouldn't need to wear a wire or install any surveillance cameras?"

"No. Once you get info to work with, you're out of there. We take it from there."

"Say I get this information when Gary goes to lunch. Afterward, how do I quit so it doesn't raise suspicion?" She didn't ask what would happen if they caught her going through his file cabinet or if she had to keep going back until they made arrests.

"You can tell him your kid is sick. Or that you're sick."

"That would explain me taking a day or two off, but what if it takes longer?"

"You can screw up so bad that they fire you. Or say you got another job. If they're involved in illegal shit, they aren't gonna ask you to do a two-week notice. *Don't* tell him you don't feel safe there. That would tip them off."

She nodded meekly. The detective made things sound easy. She didn't want to be there anymore, but what if no one at the dealership was involved? They were investigated, and Boothe told her they all had cleared with solid alibis. Her seeing the man get something out of the car was the reason they were looking at Gary now. If she quit for no reason, without another job or leads, how would she support herself and Alexis? "And if I find nothing?"

"Then I guess we're back to square one with no leads on who killed your husband."

She hated the helpless feeling washing over her. Worse, she and Alexis could be in danger. She had to do something. "I'll do it." She said it with more confidence than she felt, but she was not going to let the grumble coming from Ray or his crossed his arms intimidate her.

"I should be in the office all day tomorrow." Detective Boothe pushed to his feet. "Call me if you need anything. If you find anything."

"We need your personal cell phone number." Ray stood and towered over the older man in a showdown for power.

"Good idea." Boothe agreed more with his words than his tone or expression. He pulled out one of his cards and wrote a number on the back, then laid it on the coffee table in front of Stephanie.

"Mommy will be right back, sweetie. I'm going to show

the detective out." She took control rather than give Ray an opportunity to unload on the detective.

Showing him out alone gave Detective Boothe a chance to tell her again what he needed—and add another request. One she knew Ray would have shot down.

Now she had to tell Ray. This was not going to be fun.

"You DON'T HAVE to do this," Ray insisted.

"What choice do I have?"

"One to stay safe."

"We don't know that it will be dangerous."

"Why take the chance? What about Alexis? Us?"

"As I see it, there are three ways this can go down. First, I don't go. That means I quit my job and have no income. I can barely pay my bills now. How will I feed my daughter? The reason I can afford to stay in our house is that I'm making payments on the mortgage my parents took out over fifteen years ago. Keeping it gives Anni and Nik a home when they aren't in school." She took a deep breath to ward off the feeling of being sucked into a whirlpool. "Since I might still be seen as a threat, I won't feel safe staying in Taylors. I have nowhere to go—except to move to Finland and live with my parents." Which is what they'd tried hard to get her to do after Sam's death.

Ray's head reared back, and his eyes went wide. He hadn't thought of her moving overseas. Only his expression morphed to a more triumphant one.

"You and Alexis come with me to Fort Campbell." He looked toward Alexis playing on the floor as if to say he was all in.

Whoa. "I can't put you in that position because we slept together a few times."

"You're not putting—"

"I'm not ready." She took his hand in hers, praying he'd understand because the possibility of turning him away cut her to the soul. Her concerns about putting him in danger would only fall on deaf ears from what she'd seen. But he wasn't invincible. Nobody was.

"The second option, I do go. And if I find information that the police can use to connect Gary to a drug operation, he'll be arrested. Then I'm without a job since the dealership would close, and I could make myself a target of dangerous people."

"That's what I'm saying."

"Let me finish. The third alternative is I go, but I don't find anything—because there's nothing to find. Maybe what I saw that night was what Gary said it was, and I let my imagination run wild."

"And the men at your house the other night?" Ray's skepticism hammered at her confidence.

"Gary keeps a lot of cash in the safe sometimes. Maybe they wanted me to get them in there, thinking I could open it. It could be tied to Sam's murder."

Rather than shut her down, Ray's eyes narrowed as he contemplated that scenario.

"If Gary's on the level, I get to keep my job. Alexis and I can stay in our home. You and I can give this long-distance relationship a chance to see where it goes." She implored him with her eyes to listen. To agree. It might be working, based on his silence, so she kept going. "I'm doing this *for us*. I admit it—I'm not entirely comfortable with going back there, but Mondays are busy with customers coming in to negotiate or close deals on cars they looked at over the weekend. And there's no way everybody at the dealership would be involved. No one would risk trying anything with a bunch of witnesses around."

Ray looked somewhat mollified, but she had to tell him the rest. "On Mondays, Gary doesn't usually go out for lunch. He spends a lot of the day looking at auto auction sites for vehicles that potential customers want or to replace inventory sold over the weekend."

Ray pulled his hand free and interlocked his fingers behind his head. His long growl startled Alexis. "You're saying you'll keep going in until ..." He broke eye contact for several long seconds. "I leave Wednesday to go back to base. What if you haven't gotten a look at the files?"

"I think the safest thing is to stay late Monday. Say I need to catch up after being out Friday. After everyone has left, you can stake out the office until I'm done."

"Or you let me in to pick the locks. That sounds a hell of a lot better than trying to get into the files with people there. But would you even have to go in tomorrow?"

"If I don't, we're back to the problem of the security system recording me, and you, entering." A disgruntled sigh was the only protest he made to that point, so she continued, "And since if I go in for a day or two, then quit, that may look suspicious and derail the investigation. Boothe wants me to go in for several days to get details on incoming shipments—*if* I feel comfortable doing it."

"No. Just no. You get the information, and you're done. You can say you're quitting because you're eloping with your soldier boyfriend."

That wasn't close to the response she'd anticipated. "Right. Like they'd believe that when I haven't even mentioned any boyfriend."

"Tell them you didn't say anything about a boyfriend

because you didn't want people to judge you. Or maybe that we were messaging as friends while I was deployed, but now that I'm back, we know it's more than friends and want to be together."

"Just like that?"

"Sure. Happens in the military more than you'd believe."

He wasn't really suggesting eloping, was he? This was just a story to explain her quitting. "I'm not exactly the impulsive type."

"We've been friends for years. It's not like we have to date to get to know each other."

"Friends is a different kind of knowing each other."

"I know you're a great cook and mother. You go to church almost every Sunday. You're a peacemaker and put others before yourself. Given a choice of the beach or mountains, you'd pick the beach. You like eighties rock, and you can carry a tune, even though you don't think you sing well. You have a sweet tooth and aren't embarrassed to go for the corner piece of cake."

"Wait. How do you ...?" She stared right into his eyes. What she saw there, the naked vulnerability, the longing, made it clear this went deeper than exploring an old crush.

Here was the man she'd fantasized about being with for years, despite thinking he'd never be interested in her that way, and he'd just told her he knew her better than her family and friends. He made it sound like the values she held appealed to him. The physical attraction they shared played a role but wasn't the sole basis of their relationship. She'd been trying to keep her feelings in check, but she couldn't deny that he'd captured her heart by watching over her and making her feel safe. With how he stepped in to help with Alexis. And, now, with his words.

Where had playing it safe gotten her? Widowed, with a child, and now scary people had broken into her house.

"I pay attention to things that matter to me. To people who matter to me," he said after several long beats. "Nik wasn't the only reason I liked hanging out at your house."

"You liked to eat there, too," she teased.

"True. Because I got to sit next to you, and when your family blessed the food, I got to hold your hand," he admitted with an endearingly bashful smile.

Time for her to fess up. "I might have cooked too much food sometimes to make sure there was enough to invite you to stay." For the same reason. His compliments on their cooking had always flattered her and her mother enough that her mom hadn't minded having him stay, even though Ray ate as much as two normal people. And those fantasy-fueling fifteen seconds of her hand in his had been worth Nik's rejoinders that, though Ray liked to eat, she would not win his heart through her cooking.

"Next time I see Nik, I'm going to kick his ass."

"Hold him down so I can get a few kicks in, too." Her brother deserved it for interfering, but if things had gone differently, she wouldn't have Alexis. But they were finally getting a chance to explore where things could go.

WHY COULDN'T he bring himself to say *I love you* yet? For years, Ray had compared every female he'd dated to Stephanie—or his vision of her. None had measured up. Hell, he'd begun to fear *Stephanie* wouldn't measure up to the image he'd created. She hadn't *just* measured up. She'd raised the bar even higher. He might not have said the words, but they were just words, and he'd gotten his message across. He'd seen it in Stephanie's reaction and her response.

What he wouldn't give for his parents to call and say they were delayed or spending another night in Atlanta. Now that Stephanie realized this was more than sex, he wanted to make love to her again. They could explore this mutual attraction with their future in front of them. That outlook took the edge off the disappointment that they'd have to sleep in different beds tonight. Hand jobs had sufficed when he was deployed but held little appeal after the last two days.

With the unlocking of the deadbolt, Stephanie scrambled off the sofa to join Alexis playing with her blocks on the floor, the picture of innocence.

Ray swiveled on the sofa to face his parents. "Welcome back. Need help with the luggage?"

"I got it." His dad had his mom's overnight case slung over his shoulder and a suitcase in each hand.

His father spotted Stephanie and Alexis when he stepped through the foyer. "No news on the men who broke into your house?"

"Unfortunately, no," Stephanie said. "The detective came by earlier. He said if those men weren't locals and they got word we had their descriptions, they may have left town."

"You know you're welcome to stay here as long as necessary," Tarja said.

"Thank you, but I plan to be out of your hair tomorrow."

Ray gritted his teeth to keep from interjecting his thoughts on Stephanie going back to her house before they had this case wrapped and people in jail. She knew how he felt about her. Why put her life on the line for the police to get information to bust her boss? If she insisted on keeping up the pretense of not knowing about trafficking drugs through the dealership, she would have to also go along with his I-have-a-new-boyfriend plan to explain his constant presence.

He'd intended to use most of his accrued leave for a trip with his buddies, but tomorrow he'd contact his commanding officer to see about extending his leave a few days. It's not as if his unit had much going on, having just gotten back from Iraq. That would give him a few more days with Stephanie anyway. Cement where things were going between them.

"How was the wedding?" he asked his folks.

"Nobody objected, and they said, *I do*," his dad said with his usual dry sense of humor.

Tarja swatted his arm. "Don't listen to him. Everything was wonderful and so romantic. The family was disappointed you weren't able to come. They wanted to welcome you back from Iraq."

"I was where I needed to be." Man, was he ever, but his parents didn't need to know the details.

"I know. We explained you were helping a neighbor in trouble," his mother said.

"You told people?"

She looked surprised at his harsh tone. "What? They asked why you weren't there."

Ray ran a hand over his face. He couldn't expect his mother to understand operational security. "It's okay. The chances any of them saying anything to someone and it getting back to anyone connected to the break-in are minimal." Nothing he could do about it now.

"Oh, my," she said when she stepped further into the

family room. "You put up the bookshelves and unpacked all the boxes?" She turned to take in the room and kitchen.

"We figured we should be helpful while lying low. We didn't do your bedroom, and things may not be where you want them, but we got most everything else out of boxes," Stephanie said innocently, though Ray noticed her cheeks flush.

"Thank you. That's a tremendous help." Tarja's concerned gaze drilled into Ray. "I hope you aren't going back to our old house tonight with those men still out there."

"No. I'm staying here. I'll get some blankets and sleep on the floor. We already changed the sheets on your bed."

"You didn't need to do that."

"It's done, and the bed is made with military regulation corners." His mother looked at him as if he'd sprouted a second head. The Army had changed some of his ways.

"I've got extra bedding in the linen closet," his mother said.

"Come here, baby girl." Stephanie scooped Alexis up. "I'm going to change her for bed." She gave a nod to Ray.

He got out pillows and blankets to make a pallet on the floor, then stepped into the guest room to see what the head nod was about. "What's up?"

"She knows something is going on between us." Stephanie slipped Alexis's arms into the sleeper.

"They just walked in. How could she know?" He hadn't even touched Stephanie.

"She's intuitive. Moms pick up on that kind of thing."

"It's not like I planned on keeping us a secret." Though he wasn't going to tell his mother they had slept together— in their bed, among other places. "My parents love you. In fact, if this doesn't work out, they may keep you and disown me."

"I doubt that." She lifted Alexis.

"I'm serious. Mom says you're like the daughter she never had." He slipped an arm around her. "And she thinks of Alexis as a granddaughter. Sends me pictures of her dressed in cute outfits she can't resist buying for her." Either she liked shopping for baby stuff, or his mom had been sending him subtle hints after Sam's death.

"Maybe you should have been a pilot instead of a soldier since you like to move at five hundred miles an hour."

"I don't think waiting six years to be with the woman of my dreams is moving fast," he countered.

And he wasn't going to let siblings, parents, or even drug traffickers get in the way.

TEN

You *will not throw up. You will not throw up.*

Tarja insisted on fixing breakfast this morning, but Stephanie only managed a few bites. Now, she glanced at the bushes planted along the exterior of the dealership. If she was going to lose it, this might be a better spot than inside. Even here, though, one of the sales guys might see her, and she didn't want to explain. Worse, Ray had insisted on escorting her to drop off Alexis to make sure nobody was watching or tailing her, and he was currently parked across the street. Seeing her puke in the bushes wasn't an image she wanted burned in his brain. Besides, if he sensed weakness, it'd lead to another battle about her being here.

He promised he wouldn't sit there all day since Detective Boothe promised to have patrol and unmarked cars pass periodically. She got the feeling his assurance was directed as much at Ray as a reminder to leave this to the authorities.

If any of her coworkers noticed her being jittery, they could attribute it to the break-in at her house. However, she didn't want it to become contagious and hamper her ability to get a read on whether Gary or any of the other employees were acting suspicious or out of character.

"Stephanie, glad you're back. I heard what happened." John was the first to greet her. He left his cubicle with files in hand. "I hope you're all right. Look, I, uh, was slammed on Saturday, and I have clients coming in to pick up their new vehicle at noon and another at three. Can you get their paperwork in order?" He held out the folders with an apologetic expression.

"Sure. I'll get right on it." John had been at the dealership for over a decade, and his pool of returning customers kept him busier than other sales associates. He might hate doing financing documents, but he never asked her to make coffee.

Gary came out of his office right after she sat down at her desk.

"I wasn't sure you'd be back today. How are you doing?" The expression on his face didn't reflect what she'd call concern.

"I'm still shook up, but I can't hide forever, and I need to work. I'm trusting the police will find the men who came to my house."

"That's, uh, that's good. And you're sure you can ID these guys if the police find them?"

"*We* definitely could ID them."

A flicker of alarm crossed Gary's face with the reminder she wasn't the only one who could identify the men impersonating detectives. "Let me know if you need anything."

Now that her trust in him was shot, he'd be the last person she'd ask for help.

Stephanie sorted through the files and prioritized the work in front of her before digging in. Staying busy kept her mind off the task she dreaded. However, every time someone walked past her desk or through the dealership's front doors, she couldn't help but look.

She returned the packet of paperwork to John and went to the breakroom for coffee. She poured a cup and debated leaving the nearly empty pot behind, but after adding sugar to her cup, she caved and dumped the grounds from the basket into the trash.

"Morning, Steph. Gary told us you had some guys break into your house last week." Lonnie Blanchard lounged in the doorway. "Man, you can't catch a break, can you?"

She placed a filter in the basket, then opened a fresh packet of grounds. Rather than offer to take over or even fill the pot with water, he leaned against the counter, holding his mug imprinted with a race car.

"They say things happen in threes. One more, and you're done."

So much for compassion. "Thanks. Here." She thrust the empty coffee pot at him. "I've got a lot of work to catch up on after being out on Friday."

STEPHANIE PICKED up her cell phone and hit the redial button to touch base with Ray.

He answered on the third ring. "Hey, found anything useful?"

"No chance." So far, the day had passed as usual. "I had lunch at my desk, but so did he. Looking like plan B." The only time Gary had come out of his office was to get more coffee or hit the bathroom. And today, he'd kept the door closed unless one of the salesmen went in to consult him. Even though she routinely entered Gary's office, it looked like she'd have to attempt to access the file cabinet after hours, when there'd be no one around to catch her snooping through his files.

"Okay. I'm taking the last load of stuff from my parents' house to the condo, but—"

"Hang on," she said when the office line rang. "Good afternoon. Floyd's Fine Motors. How can I help you?"

"Stephanie Anderson?"

"Yes." Detective Boothe's voice made hope swell that he had good news.

"I wanted to see if you had any information for me," he said.

She checked to see if anyone was within earshot. "No. I haven't had a chance to, uh, complete that form yet. Do you have updates on your end?"

"Afraid we haven't gotten any matches, even with the pictures from the video." His words were like a dart popping the balloon of hope she clung to. "Looks like the carrier is our best shot at some leads."

"I should have that information tonight." *Should* being the operative word. She hung up and switched back to her cell phone. "Sorry, that was ..."

"I heard. I was hoping he would have good news. What happens if Gary stays late tonight? You're not staying there alone with him under *any* circumstances." Ray's voice took on a chilling do-not-buck-me-on-this tone.

"I know." She was taking enough chances, but she had too much to live for. Not only did she have Alexis, but now she had hope for a future with Ray. "I love—that you worry about me."

"I'd rather have no reason to worry," he responded, with a hint of disappointment in his voice.

Had it been a Freudian slip? She hadn't planned to say the L-word. Trying to cover probably made it worse.

Maybe she should have gone ahead and said it. But what if she was confusing his protecting her with other emotions? Until she knew if they had any chance at a future, it wasn't fair to say she loved him and risk breaking both their hearts if she had to leave the country. Alexis had to come first.

"I'll be there before six, and we'll roll with it."

"Thank you."

———

"Stephanie." Lonnie stood in the opening to her cubicle. "I need you to take me to pick up a car."

"What?" She checked the clock on the wall.

"I have a guy who's way past due on payments. I caught up with his ex, who's also on the loan, and she told me where he's keeping the car. I need to pick it up."

"I've got work to do." The last thing she wanted was to leave now.

"John's got clients, and we need someone available for walk-ins. That leaves you."

"Can Gary go?" That would be ideal.

"*Pff.* Right. Gary said to have *you* drive, and that you can go home for the day after you drop me off."

The idea that Gary didn't want her here sent chills racing through her. Did he suspect anything, or was it truly coincidence? They typically did a few repos a year. How the hell could she get out of this without explaining?

"Can you give me ten minutes to finish this file?"

"That can wait. I need to be gone before this guy gets home." He gave her a hurry-up wave.

"Let me go to the bathroom first." He couldn't object to that. "Why don't you start my car. It takes the AC a while to cool down." She dug out her keys and forced them in his hand, then beelined to the bathroom.

Once she closed the door, she took a few deep breaths to regain her composure. Should she try to come back after and then stay, or try again tomorrow? Could she convince Ray? *Crap.* Why did this have to come up now?

She couldn't leave without letting someone know. She dialed Detective Boothe, figuring he'd be the most supportive. It rang through to his office voicemail. *No. Not now.* She left a brief message, but now her heart was racing more than before, and sweat broke out all over her body. *Calm down.* She tried his cell. *Come on, come on.* Shit! Again, her call went to voicemail. She left a slightly more panicked message there.

Lonnie wasn't going to wait forever, and she didn't need him pounding on the door or overhearing. She had no other choice.

Her fear dropped a notch when Ray answered. "Hey. Change of plans. They need me to go with one of the sales guys to repossess a car."

"No. Wait. Why you?"

"Because the sales guys bring in money and I'm just admin. I've gone before." One time. She went with John, and it had broken her heart to see the single grandma taking care of her grandbabies plead for more time to make a payment. "Look, I'll see if I can come back. If that doesn't work, we'll have to go with tomorrow."

"On two conditions." Ray's voice was akin to a growl. "Leave your phone on so I can hear what's happening—turn it to max volume and don't bury it in your purse. Secondly, get him to tell you where you're going."

"Fine. Hang on." She adjusted the settings before slipping the phone in the outside pocket with the microphone facing out. "Testing, one, two, three." She sounded like an idiot, but if it made Ray happy, she could live with it. "Could you hear me okay?"

"Yes." Based on the drawn-out word, he still wasn't happy.

She put the phone back in her purse. This might be a boring hour for Ray, but she had to get this over with.

As she headed out the front door, Lonnie met her on his way back in. "There you are. Geez, what took so long? Let's go. I'll drive."

"I don't think so." She blocked him from opening the driver's side door of *her* car.

"I know where we're going."

"Great. You can navigate."

"Whatever. Just trying to be helpful." He went around to the passenger side.

She adjusted the radio's volume and turned the air conditioner fan down a few notches to make it quieter inside the car.

"Take a left out of the parking lot."

"Where are we going? I probably need to get gas." She stalled as she set her purse on the armrest between them.

"It's only about ten miles." He leaned over to see the gas gauge on the dash. "You should be good." He picked up her purse and moved to put it in the back.

"Uh, let me have that, please."

He rolled his eyes and handed her the purse.

She reached inside, fished around, and came up with a mint. Now, where to put the purse so Ray could hear, yet Lonnie wouldn't be suspicious? She tucked it between her and the door, hoping Ray could hear Lonnie from there.

She popped the mint in her mouth and began to back out. "Tell me where I'm going."

"Don't worry. I've got directions." Lonnie kept his gaze straight ahead. The fingers on his left hand drummed on his thigh.

That wasn't going to cut it. "What's with not telling me? Are you taking me someplace sketchy I wouldn't want to go?" She didn't have a choice but to play the timid female if she was going to pry information out of Lonnie.

"No, I'm not taking you to the west end of Greenville." He shook his head. "Head toward 253."

It wasn't an exact location, but she'd given Ray an idea of the direction they were going. They'd gone about a mile when Lonnie pulled his cigarette packet from his shirt pocket and tapped one out.

"You're not smoking in my car."

"I'll hold it outside." He put the cigarette between his lips.

"No! I don't want the smoke smell in my car. Period." Lonnie already ranked as her least favorite of the salesman at the dealership, and he wasn't earning any points today. Sam hadn't liked the guy either. He might treat her like a dumb blonde, but this was her car, and she was putting her foot down—on the brake and ordering him out if he went ahead and lit the damn cigarette.

"Come on. Just a few puffs," he pleaded, squinting at her in an intimidating fashion, but she refused to back down. Ray should be proud of her assertiveness.After a few seconds, Lonnie huffed a sigh and put the cigarette behind his ear like something out of a fifties movie.

When he reached to mess with the radio, she blocked him. "I like this song." Silence would be major-league uncomfortable, but she couldn't risk him cranking it up, making it impossible for Ray to hear.

The longer they rode, the twitchier Lonnie got. They

were out in the boondocks. She'd lived in this area her whole life and had never been out here.

"Are you sure we didn't miss a turn?"

"Don't think so. He's keeping the car someplace he, uh, thinks we won't find it."

Hadn't Lonnie said they needed to get there before the guy got home? Now he was saying it was someplace else? The further they drove, her fear grew that she'd made a bad decision to come with Lonnie. "It would help if you told me street names so I could look, too."

He hesitated, looking at the scrap of paper in his hand. "I think it's Arbor Lane."

"Did you say Arbor or Harbor?" she repeated for Ray's benefit. She doubted he knew any of these backwoods roads, but she was beginning to understand why he'd wanted to listen in.

Damn it. He should have stayed and kept an eye on the dealership rather than follow Detective Boothe's orders to leave surveillance to the police.

Stephanie hadn't managed to get an exact destination out of Lonnie, but she was doing a good job getting street names to him. Ray tried to type the last name that she fed him into the GPS while careening down the winding, unfamiliar road. The moving box he hadn't unloaded slid across the truck bed as he overcorrected to get back into his lane—as if it mattered out here in the middle of bumfuck nowhere.

The best he could tell, he was only five to seven minutes from their location. He didn't want to risk trying a three-way call to Detective Boothe, in case it caused him to miss her next clue on where to turn.

He couldn't help but jump to the worst-case scenario. Sam's killer was still out there, and suspicious shit pointed to the dealership being connected. Drugs and money made people do stupid and dangerous things. Being a protector was hardwired into his DNA, and Stephanie's involvement made it personal. Very personal. What could Detective Boothe do? Arrest him for trying to protect Stephanie?

He was pissed Boothe even asked her to go back there to dig up info. He was pissed Stephanie would be sent along to repo the car of a guy desperate enough to hide it. He was pissed at the misogynistic way Lonnie treated Stephanie.

But mostly, he was pissed at himself for letting her go back at all.

Why the fuck did she go with this jackass? Had it seemed better than staying at the dealership with Gary? Stephanie was too trusting, even naive. He, on the other hand, had experienced enough bad shit in Iraq that "skeptical" should be his middle name. Stephanie driving into the sticks with this jackass gave him the sensation of fire ants swarming all over his body. Similar to the feeling he'd gotten when someone easily shared where to find insurgents or weapons caches. He'd learned to look deeper to see if they had a motive. Like sending them into an ambush.

Nothing about this felt right. He debated hanging up and calling back to tell her to stop following this clown's directions and drive someplace populated. What if she didn't answer? He couldn't risk it.

To hell with orders to leave it to the police. He'd be two feet from Stephanie's bumper if he could intercept them.

"Slow down." Lonnie's voice broke the brief silence. "The road should be coming up."

Every word the guy said to Stephanie made Ray want to give him a lesson on how to treat a woman. A lesson that would involve blood or make Lonnie piss himself. He held the phone back to his ear, waiting for the street name.

"Turn here."

"Are you sure? That's not even a street. What good is a car if he has to hide it down some dirt road so far out he can't use it?"

"Hell if I know. But that's what it says."

Ray's panic grew as the background noise changed from the hum of tires on asphalt to the uneven cadence of tires on a rutted dirt road.

"This doesn't feel right. Let me see those directions." Something in the change in Stephanie's tone of voice set off warning sirens in Ray's head.

ELEVEN

Her tires skidded on the gravel, and dust billowed when Stephanie braked to a stop. She snatched the paper from Lonnie's hand.

The writing on the paper was unmistakably *Gary's* scrawl.

No wonder the pieces Lonnie had told her did not fit in this puzzle.

Gary had been the most in-your-face suspect, but it hadn't occurred to her that anyone else would be involved. *Shit.* What could she do when she was so far from anyone or anywhere? She needed confirmation.

"We aren't out here to pick up a car, are we?" she asked with fateful certainty.

"Of course we are." Lonnie's voice wavered. "Why would you say that?"

"Because I figured out someone was using the cars bought at auction to transport drugs via the delivery carrier. I didn't suspect you were involved. Until now." No point in going for subtle.

"I, uh ... what?" Lonnie gave a nervous laugh. "Wow. You really don't think much of me, do you?"

"Not if you're involved in smuggling or distributing drugs."

"I don't know where this is coming from." His timbre shifted to the smooth-talking manner he used when trying to convince a customer he was giving them a great deal on a used car.

She wasn't buying it. "Did Sam find out, too? Is that why you killed him?"

"Whoa! I didn't have anything to do with that. I—" He stopped himself. "Let's cut the crazy talk and get this over with." He motioned for her to keep going.

If she went to the end of this road with Lonnie, that would be the end for her. For Alexis's sake, she had to be brave.

"Everyone at the dealership knows I left with you. The police are already looking into Gary, and I called the police station when I was in the bathroom." She saw the dawning of how screwed he was on his face and kept going. "Sergeant Lundgren knows I left with you, too. If something happens to me, the person they look at will one hundred percent be *you*." Time for her to sell it. "Right now, you're looking at what, drug trafficking? You can cut a deal with the detectives if you tell them who's distributing the drugs. And who murdered Sam. Don't make this worse for yourself."

"If only it were that easy." Lonnie produced a scary-looking compact black gun from behind his back. "Keep driving."

Oh. Holy. Shit! "Wh-what are you going to do? Shoot me?" She prayed Ray was still listening—though what could he do? "You'll have to shoot me here because I *am not* walking to some shallow grave. What then? Drag my body off into the woods? Is Gary going to—"

"Shut up! I can't think!"

"—come pick you up, or are you going to drive off in my car? Sitting in my blood? Don't you see, you'll never get away with this. Your best option is to go to the police, and you give them names to put the people responsible in jail."

"You don't know these people. If I don't do what they want ..."

"So, instead, you'll sacrifice me? Can you live with your-self if you kill me and make my daughter an orphan? You'll be on the run for the rest of your life."

Desperation and despair overtook his countenance. He knew he had no good options, and that made him danger-ous. Even deadly.

"It's the only shot I've got. I didn't want it to turn out this way." His thumb moved over the top of the gun. "Drive to the end of the road."

She cringed at the *click*, signaling her failure to reach any remaining scrap of humanity. If she could just make it back to the road. The only move she had left entailed almost as great a risk as Lonnie with a gun, but she wasn't going to make it easy. And if she was going to meet her Creator today, maybe she could send Lonnie to hell early.

She pressed the gas, cranked the wheel, and swung the car, trying to turn on the narrow road.

Lonnie lunged for the wheel.

TWELVE

S *hoot her?* The bastard had a gun? As much as Ray wanted that to be an offhand comment, everything Stephanie had said with Lonnie had the added layer of relaying information. She wouldn't have said that flippantly. Her next comment cemented it. This was one time he wished his instincts had not been right. Why had he let her go?

His rage grew, and his nerves jangled like they were connected to a live wire. Lonnie was not a foreign insurgent, but threatening Stephanie made him Ray's enemy. Lonnie might have a weapon, but so did he—and he knew damn well how to use it. He *would* kill to protect Stephanie. It may result in a dishonorable discharge or jail time, but he'd do it. Without hesitation.

As he reached under his seat and grabbed his M11 Sig from the mount, he floored the accelerator. He already had his phone at max volume, but Ray strained to hear the asshole's reply to Stephanie's attempts to talk some sense into him.

Don't listen to him, babe. Don't do it. Don't you dare go where he's telling you.

What the hell was going on? He couldn't make out words. More like grunts and movement. He envisioned a struggle before there was a gunshot, and the unmistakable crunch of metal and shattering of glass, followed by the wounded blaring of the car horn.

"Stephanie! Stephanie, can you hear me!"

He fought the instinct to hang up and call 9-1-1 only because he didn't have an address to give them yet. He had to be close. He scanned the road ahead of him, looking for a turnoff that could be what she had described. Out of the corner of his eye, he saw a dirt path off the road as he passed it. He stomped on the brakes, then slammed the gear into reverse before the truck even stopped. Looking over his shoulder as he backed up, he noted the chalk mark on the tree. The same technique they used in Iraq to discreetly mark locations. Adrenaline surged through him. This had to be it.

He turned down the phone volume and lowered the window. He made out the sound of the horn. It was the years of training that kept him from racing down there, kicking up dust, and announcing his invasion to get to Stephanie.

The horn grew louder. The blare filled the truck cab and worked its way into his soul. *Please, God, don't let me be too late.*

A wisp of gray smoke rolled toward him a second before the back of Stephanie's car came into view off the road. The front was buried in the brush, and the passenger side smashed against the trunk of one of the towering pine trees lining the dirt road.

Ray came to a stop ten feet away, angling his truck

across the road. He took the time to do a scan of the area before emerging from his vehicle. Gun in hand with the safety off, he approached the vehicle, his eyes on the two figures in the front seats. Stephanie's head slumped against the drivers' side window.

Neither occupant moved.

He opened Stephanie's door, and her head lolled without so much as a whimper, but the seatbelt held her in place. He couldn't miss the spreading pool of blood in her lap. "Oh, God."

Though he ached to pull her out to triage immediately, he couldn't risk it yet. He pressed his fingers to her neck and found a faint pulse. Hate poured from every cell as he canvassed the scene and located the weapon on the floorboard near Lonnie's feet—where there was no way Ray could reach it. He eased back Stephanie's seat.

Lonnie moaned, and his head rolled back. His eyes flickered open, and his gaze roamed unsteadily, then paused on Ray. "Help me."

In your dreams, asshole. Ray locked his jaw and unfastened Stephanie's seatbelt. A smear of her blood stained his arm.

Lonnie slowly became more cognizant of his predicament and tried to open his door. "I can't get out," he slurred. He touched a hand to his head, then stared at the blood on it from the cut on his head.

"I have to get her out. What happened?"

"She hit the tree."

Duh! "She's bleeding a lot," Ray said through his gritted teeth to keep from saying what he wanted to say. He needed to focus on Stephanie and not waste time on this bastard. "There's a lot of glass. Sit tight."

Ray eased her into his arms, doing his best to support

her head and not aggravate any injuries. With the car smoking, he laid her on the ground a safe distance away. He knelt to evaluate her injuries, and it only took a few seconds to find the bullet hole above her right hip. Blood seeped out with each heartbeat. *Hang in there, babe.*

She needed help. ASAP. He quickly prioritized his action plan. 9-1-1. Stop, or at least slow, the bleeding. Kill Lonnie.

Since there wasn't an address, he gave the emergency dispatcher the GPS coordinates as well as the cross street names. They were so freaking far out in the country. What if an ambulance couldn't get here in time? "I need you to send a MEDEVAC chopper." He didn't know where the hell it could land, but the sooner she got into surgery, the better.

"I can't authorize that," the dispatcher said in a maddeningly calm manner. "When the medics arrive, they'll make that call."

"That may be too late. She has a gunshot wound in her lower abdomen and is losing a lot of blood. She's been unconscious for several minutes. Her pulse is weak and thready." He used terms he recalled hearing from Ewkonu, his team's medic, hoping to convince the woman he wasn't being overdramatic.

"The ambulance has been dispatched. ETA is approximately sixteen minutes. I need you to stay on the line with me," she requested, not backing down an inch.

Damn it! She might not be able to authorize it, but Detective Boothe might have some sway. Sixteen minutes was too damn long. Ray dashed back to the car to get Stephanie's phone.

In the car, Lonnie had unbuckled his seat belt and was reaching for the gun.

Oh, fuck no. Ray hit his phone's mute button and dove inside. "Let me help you." He pressed a hand to Lonnie's chest and shoved him back. With his free hand, he groped on the floor until he got a hold of the weapon, then backed out of the car.

"Where are you going?" Lonnie's eyes pleaded for help, and he shifted as if to navigate his way over the gear shift to get out.

"You shot her. If you step out of this car, I. Will. Shoot. You." Ray looked him dead in the eye. "I just got back from Iraq, so when I say you'll be in the morgue rather than facing prison time, I'm not messing around. You decide, asshole."

He half-wanted him to try. Lonnie's face went pale before he slouched in the seat. Ray waited a moment before he scooped up Stephanie's purse from the ground where it had fallen, then and slammed the door shut.

The only signs of life from Stephanie were the slight rise and fall of her chest. Fighting against panic, he dumped her bag upside down, spilling the contents onto the dirt. He snatched up her phone, going straight to the call record and redialing the detective.

While it rang, a white and pink wrapper caught his eye. Could it be …? He grabbed it and ripped off the plastic covering. Yes! Guys on his team had made fun of Ekwonu for carrying tampons in his medic kit, but he swore they'd saved soldiers' lives. *Please, Lord, let this work.*

THIRTEEN

Ray barely refrained from ambushing the surgeon who'd come out to give another family news on their loved one. Hadn't he been here longer than them? His experience in the Army should have him used to waiting around with nothing happening, but this was torture.

He pulled out his phone at the text notification. This time it was Nik saying he got stuck in road construction traffic. Even though he didn't have an update, Ray called his parents, who were as worried as he was.

"No news yet. She's still in surgery," Ray told his mom, wishing he could give her reassurances. Wishing someone would reassure *him* that Stephanie was going to pull through. "How's Alexis?"

"She's asking for mommy, but she ate, and your dad and I took her for a walk. I'm about to give her a bath and put her to bed."

"Thanks for taking care of her."

"Of course. Dad said he could bring you dinner and sit with you."

"No, that's okay. I can't eat. Nik should be here soon, anyway."

"All right. Let us know as soon as you know more."

"Will do." Ray hung up and settled back to pray and wait.

He looked up each time someone entered the waiting room. When he finally saw Nik rushing toward him, his face a mask of panic and concern, Ray stood to face his friend.

"How is she?" Nik demanded.

"Still in surgery. They gave me an update when I got here, but no word since. Did you call Anni?"

"Not yet. I wanted to have more details. I'll call her and my parents once I know ..."

"Yeah." Thank God Boothe had come through in trusting Ray's assessment and ordered the MEDEVAC team who arrived minutes after the medics. Stephanie had been so pale when they'd loaded her, and they hadn't let Ray ride in the chopper. He'd clung to the fact she was alive and in good hands. Then the cops had questioned him, which detained him further. He'd been a wreck by the time he'd gotten to the hospital.

She'd made it here. From what the surgical nurse had told him, it was bad, but the surgeon was hopeful he could stop the bleeding.

It'd been hours now.

"What the hell happened?"

Now would be a really good time for the doctor to come give them good news. The doors to the surgical wing didn't open, so Ray motioned to the chairs and sank back into his seat. It took a good twenty minutes to fill Nik in, not sparing any details even though Ray feared he might lose Stephanie and his former best friend in a span of a few hours.

"Damn it. Why didn't she listen to you?" Nik's comment eased some of Ray's self-incrimination. "They questioned everyone at the dealership after Sam's murder, but they told us they all had alibis. Had you met Lonnie?"

"No, and neither she nor the detective ever mentioned him. Guess that's why."

"I met him a couple of times. Sam never liked him. Said he was the type of liar who gave used car salesmen a bad rap. But this ..."

"He won't hurt her ever again," Ray promised.

FOURTEEN

When Stephanie stirred, Ray got to his feet and hovered over the hospital bed. Her eyes fluttered but stayed open, and her mouth curved into a smile as she focused on his face.

"I'm alive."

"Yes, you *are*." He wasn't going to tell her how close she had come to dying. He'd had his doubts waiting for both the MEDEVAC chopper and for her to get out of surgery. Her face was pale even after the blood transfusions they'd given her, but the surgeon had assured them she was out of the woods.

"Alexis. I have to get her." She attempted to push off the bed.

"She's fine." He put a hand on her shoulder. "Your friend, Renee, took her home from day care, and my parents have her now."

Nik stepped to the other side of the bed. "We'll take care of Alexis."

"Nik? What are you doing here?"

"I called and told him what happened," Ray said.

Stephanie aimed a loopy scowl and waved a wobbly finger in Nik's direction. "I'm mad as hell at you."

"Me? What'd I do?" a surprised Nik asked.

"You said he couldn't date me." She pointed toward Ray. "And told me he didn't want to."

Nik laughed. "Fine. You're right. I was an immature ass. I didn't want to lose my best friend if you two dated and then broke up. Dolph here already told me you two are together, and I have to deal with it."

"Don't call me Dolph again, or I *will* kick your ass," Ray said in a menacing tone that made Nik laugh.

"We *should* kick his ass," she mumbled. "You hold him down for me. I won my last fight."

STEPHANIE WOKE to the feeling of déjà vu. Ray was here, immediately taking hold of her hand not encumbered with an IV.

"Hey there, beautiful." He gave her a smile that lacked authenticity.

"*Äidin oma suloinen tytär.*" Her mother's soothing voice calling her sweet girl was a medicine of its own.

"*Äiti!* How did you get here already?" It took a full day of traveling to get here from Finland.

"I caught the first flight out yesterday morning," her mother replied.

"What day is it?"

"Wednesday afternoon," Ray answered.

Wednesday? Two days had passed? "Alexis?"

"She's with my mom."

"But she's—"

"Don't worry," Ray reassured her. "I think Mom's got

Alexis calling her Nana already, and they're having a blast. Now, your mom's here to help, too. Leave her to us. *You* need to heal."

He was right. Alexis was in good hands. But another realization made her panic. "You're supposed to be back at work. Won't you get in trouble?"

"I'm not AWOL. I told them my fiancée was injured, and I needed the rest of the week off."

"Fiancée?"

"I figured it carried more weight to get the time off if I said fiancée." He winked. "I may be jumpin' the gun a little, but I'm hoping you don't dump me." He rubbed his thumb over her hand and squeezed.

Most people would say it was too early to talk marriage, but after years of knowing each other, years of dreaming up romantic scenarios, why wait months to prove to others what she knew in her heart? She wanted Ray at her side. Helping to raise her daughter and their children.

"I have no plans on dumping you. And Nik doesn't have a say."

"I already told him. Quite explicitly. After you said we were going to kick his ass," Ray said and laughed.

"When did I do that?"

"Nik was here when you woke up yesterday, and you set him straight."

"Nik was here?" A fuzzy memory came back to her. "Why did you come, Mom?" It seemed a long way to come for a hospital visit.

Her mom hesitated. "You're going to need someone to take care of you and Alexis for a while."

"Why?"

"Do you remember what happened?" Ray asked.

"Vaguely." Though she didn't want to remember the

terrors of that afternoon, she sketched out what she did recall. "I was trying to talk Lonnie into going to the police, but he pulled a gun. I was trying to turn the car around, and he grabbed for the wheel." Then her memory ended.

Ray and her mom met each other's gaze. Several seconds of weighted silence passed between them.

"What am I missing?"

The two didn't break eye contact at Stephanie's question.

"Let me tell her." Ray's tone was somber.

"Is she ready, though?" The hesitation in her mom's voice added to the apprehension swirling in the small room.

Ray gave an uncertain wobble of his head. "She needs to know."

What if ...? No! "You said Alexis was okay." If anything happened to—

"She's fine."

Thank you, God. "Tell me." Whatever it was, she could live with it if Alexis was okay. "Was Lonnie killed when I crashed the car?" If so, too damn bad. *Try and charge me.*

"No. The son of a bitch got off light with a concussion, cuts, and a few contusions. He was treated, then transferred to county lockup. Gary's in jail, too."

That news brought some relief, but didn't explain what had her mom and Ray so worried.

"You were shot." Ray held tight to her hand.

"Shot? No, I ..." She looked down her sheet-draped body, then closed her eyes to focus on what she felt. What she remembered. Why didn't she remember anything after wrestling for control of the car? Slowly, she became aware of the dull throb in her abdomen. No, lower.

"What happened?" Fear, different than she'd experienced in the car with Lonnie, but nearly as strong, made her tremble.

"The bullet entered above your right hip," Ray said.

She wiggled her toes and felt reassured when they moved on both feet.

"The surgeon said Ray saved your life." Her mother stared at him like he was a hero. Stephanie's hero.

"I just slowed the bleeding."

"And demanded they send a helicopter."

"You were losing a lot of blood because of your injury." Ray paused. A flicker of grief crossed his face before he regained control. "There was a lot of damage. The surgeon tried to stop the bleeding, but the only way to do it—" He swallowed. "They had to do a hysterectomy."

"A hysterectomy? But I'm—then I can't—" It couldn't be true. Not the thing she wanted most in life.

"I'm sorry. If I—"

"No," she cut Ray off. "It's not your fault." *She'd* insisted on going back to the dealership, never imagining a worst-case scenario. Ray and her mother stayed silent while she struggled to process this loss. She raged at the injustice on top of everything else she'd endured. It only took a moment for darkness to try to claim her. She remembered the stages of grief. Was still cycling through it from Sam's death. Getting stuck in denial wouldn't change it. "I can't give you kids," she started before the tears choked her.

"I wanted that for you. For us. But it doesn't change how I feel." Ray tugged on her hand and leaned into her field of vision. "I love you, Stephanie. There are other ways to have family. But as long as I have you and Alexis, that's enough for me."

Icy darkness suffocated her, and she couldn't speak. But Ray's warm hand held hers like a lifeline, making her realize this wasn't *worst-case*. Lonnie would have killed her. Except she'd fought. She'd survived. Maybe her future would look different than she'd envisioned, but she had a future. She had Alexis—the best part of her life. She didn't *have* to have a van full of kids. This time she'd have Ray to help her get through the grief.

She could grieve, but she would not let this destroy her.

FIFTEEN

Ray's phone rang seconds after he sent the text to Stephanie asking if it was too late to call. He kept his eyes on the road and answered. "Hey, beautiful."

"It's *never* too late to call me," she said in a way that drew visions of her smiling up at him. "And I don't expect you to ditch your buddies to call me. You're allowed a night out."

"I didn't end up going out with them." He eased into the surprise. "I wanted to warn you the truck about to pull into your drive is me."

"Really?" The excitement in her voice made his smile spread. "You didn't go AWOL, did you?"

"No. Didn't have to after all. Yesterday, Captain Barden got the full scoop on what happened and how you helped the cops get information on the drug smuggling operation. It changed his mind on letting me have leave again this weekend." The captain had also told him disobeying the detective's orders was the right thing to do in that situation, and he even recommended Ray put in for Ranger School and consider Selection for Special Operations. Exciting possibilities, but things he'd have to discuss with Stephanie first.

When he pulled into the driveway, the porch light was on and the front door open to welcome him. He stepped inside, and it felt like coming home. Not the house—her.

He dropped his duffle bag to sweep her into his arms. She definitely felt stronger as she drew his head close and kissed him as if it'd been months instead of weeks since he'd last held her. God, he loved everything about this woman. Everything was easy. Right. Even though they talked on the phone for hours every night while they were apart, it wasn't enough.

When he set Stephanie down, he studied her in the light. Her color was back to normal, and her cheeks had filled out, probably due to her mother's cooking the past few weeks since her release from the hospital.

She studied him right back. "I have to say, Sergeant Lundgren, you look pretty amazing in this uniform." She ran a hand over his arm to his chest.

"And you look totally amazing in your jammies." He slid a hand down her back to cup her butt through the lavender sleep boxers and peeked down the V-neck top. "I didn't take time to change. Hit the road right from post. Even ate dinner in the truck so I could get here—to you." He placed his other hand over hers and held it near his heart.

"Well, this is the best surprise I've had in—" She thought for a moment. "Mmm, I'd have to say in forever."

"Really? That's putting a little pressure on me to top it." Though he had every intention of doing just that.

With Gary and Lonnie under arrest, the dealership was closed, probably permanently. According to Detective Boothe, Lonnie confessed to setting up the initial drug drops, and at a minimum, they'd convict him for assault in Stephanie's shooting. Maybe even attempted murder. Gary confessed he'd received a small kickback for ordering the cars from Miami.

By helping cover up evidence in Sam's murder, Lonnie and Gary had gotten themselves neck-deep with the smuggling operation and would face related charges. No evidence emerged showing Sam's involvement—a possibility that had crossed Ray's mind. Sam probably thought he had a potential customer shopping for a car after hours and interfered with the pickup. Thank God, Stephanie hadn't met the same fate.

Boothe felt Stephanie was no longer viewed as a threat, and there was no reason for her to testify. As long as Lonnie didn't flake out on testifying, authorities should be able to convict the major players in this East Coast cocaine-smuggling operation. Still, Ray wanted her out of Taylors. He couldn't rule out they'd want retribution because she had survived the attempts on her life.

Her parents could rent or sell the house in Taylors. He could provide a place for Stephanie and Alexis to live. She could find a job around Fort Campbell easier than in Finland. No way was she moving there if he had a say. She was smart and independent and resilient. Great qualities for a military wife. He'd talked to her mother and then her father to assure them his plan wasn't a whim, and he intended to sell her on the idea this weekend.

Or maybe right now.

He brought her right hand to his lips. "Your hand's kind of bare." He rubbed his thumb over her ring finger. She'd taken off her engagement ring and wedding band the day they'd brought her home from the hospital, and she hadn't put them back on, which he took as a good sign.

"It didn't feel right to wear them any longer."

He nodded. "I think I might be able to do something about that." He reached into the side pocket of his uniform pants and drew out the ring box.

Stephanie let out a whisper of a gasp, and her mouth hung open. His excitement built as she met his eyes for several heartbeats before she reached to lift the top of the blue velvet box.

"Oh, my ... Is this ...?"

He dropped to one knee. "I know it's soon, but when you know, you know. I have no doubt I want you as my wife. I want to be a father to Alexis. I promise to do my best to provide for you, keep you safe and happy. Stephanie Laakso Anderson, will you marry me?"

Tears shimmered in her beautiful blue eyes. Her head bobbed several times. "Yes. Yes. Yes!" She tugged his hand to pull him back to his feet and placed her hands on either side of his face. "I love you," she whispered with consuming intensity, then kissed him long and hard, leaving them both breathless.

He stopped her when she started to peel apart the fasteners on his uniform. "Not here. Your mom might hear. And I have to put this on you." He took the ring out of the box and slid it onto her finger. "I hope you like it."

"It's gorgeous." She turned her hand toward the light to watch the diamond sparkle. "You could have given me a diamond chip, and I still would have said yes."

"What do you think about eloping instead of planning a wedding that's months from now?" He picked up his bag and led her to the bedroom.

"How soon?"

"As soon as we get a license. After we're married, I can apply for married housing, and you and Alexis can join me as soon as a slot opens. I'm tired of this long-distance stuff."

"Already?" She grinned at him as he set his bag down and removed his uniform jacket.

"Hell, yes. I want to be with you. *Every* day. Be the one to help with Alexis. Don't you think we've waited long enough to be together?"

"I do. I do." She pulled back the sheet on the bed and slid in.

"That's what I want to hear," he said, stripping off his shirt.

"Take off your boots, soldier, and get in bed."

Now that was an order he'd follow without question.

THANK YOU for reading *Desperate Choices*! I hope you loved getting to know Ray and Stephanie in this prequel novella for my Bad Karma Special Ops series. You'll get to see more of them in the rest of the series and meet the other heroes of the Bad Karma Special Ops team—whose love lives are as dangerous as their missions.

I appreciate your help in spreading the word about my books. Tell a friend. Share on social media. Post a review on Amazon, Goodreads, BookBub, or your favorite book site. Reviews are like hugs to authors, and I love hugs. Higher numbers of reviews will help other readers find me and know if this book is for them. It doesn't even have to be a five-star review—though those are certainly welcome and what I strive for. I don't want to disappoint my readers, so I spend time researching and hire editors. We're human though and miss things. So, if you find mistakes and want to tell me in a nice way (not like the perfectionist family member that takes glee in pointing out errors,) email me so I can fix it and I will be grateful!

And I'd love for you to join my newsletter list so you'll hear about new releases, sales, giveaways, and receive EXCLUSIVE content!

Sign up on my website: https://tracybrody.com.

The first full-length book in the Bad Karma Special Ops series is *Deadly Aim* and it was a four-time RWA® Golden Heart® finalist. Next up are *A Shot Worth Taking* and *In the Wrong Sights* — both Golden Heart Winners. They are stand alone novels with a common cast of characters, but reading them in order eliminates spoilers. I hope you'll fall in love with the leads in these books as well.

Turn the page to read an excerpt from *Deadly Aim*.

DEADLY AIM EXCERPT

Colombia, South America

Training mission, my ass.

Kristie Donovan banked her Army Black Hawk and pushed the helicopter to max speed. Now wasn't the time for her *I-knew-it* moment over her suspicions that there was more to this assignment than being sent to train Colombian Army pilots on the electronic instrument systems in their newer Sikorski UH-60 Black Hawks as they'd been told.

Command radioing in new orders mid-flight to pick up a "package with wounded" had Black Ops written all over it. Especially when the new coordinates took them right into the heart of an area known for cocaine production. Army "need to know" at its best.

"How far to the LZ?" she asked her Colombian co-pilot trainee.

Josué checked the GPS. "Thirty klicks. If I am right, this is not what you call 'landing zone.'"

"Meaning...?" Even in the tropical heat and in full uniform, goosebumps erupted down her arms.

"Like sixty-meter clearing."

"You use it for practice?" She could hope.

"Never."

"But helicopters use it?"

"Small ones owned by cartel."

Josué might be a fairly new pilot, but he knew the players here and his wide, unblinking expression as he stared told her more than she wanted to know about who used this clearing. And what for. Great. *Let's use a drug lord's landing pad. I'm sure he won't mind. He might even send a welcoming committee—a well-armed one.*

Sixty meters—if the jungle hadn't encroached. Drops of sweat trickled down her neck the closer they flew to their target.

She pulled back on the cyclic controller and slowed the helicopter. The blur of the jungle below came into focus. She leaned forward, her gaze sweeping left to right through the front windscreen at the terrain below. Nothing but trees, trees, and more trees. The thick veil of green hid anything, or anyone, on the ground.

"Do you see the LZ?" she asked her crew chief and gunner.

"Negative," they both reported from their vantage points on either side of the aircraft.

"We're not giving anyone extra time to make us a target. Not in daylight." She keyed the radio mic. "Ghost Rider One-Three to Bad Karma, come in." She attempted to hail their package on the ground.

No response.

Energy drained from her limbs as she envisioned the scenario that would keep them from answering. "Ghost Rider One-Three to Bad Karma, come in." Silence saturated the air. They weren't too late. She refused to—

"Ghost Rider One-Three, this is Bad Karma Two-One. We have a visual on you. Popping smoke."

Thank God. She let out the breath she hadn't realized she'd been holding.

The Bad Karma radioman's perfect English screamed American. Yeah, no doubt left now that this mission was covert, classified, and maybe even suicidally dangerous.

"I see them." Josué pointed to where a thin smoke trail pinpointed their location.

Kristie banked left.

"Be advised, we have tangos inbound," the radioman reported, "and one friendly in their vicinity."

"You've got to be kidding me," she muttered. *Why the hell was he not with his team?* Her gunner couldn't deal with the tangos if they might hit one of their own.

She ground her teeth as the answer came to her. Someone *special* volunteered to do something incredibly brave—or incredibly stupid—to protect his team. Exactly the way Eric would have done. Had done.

Her throat constricted, and her eyes burned. She pressed against the seat. *Breathe, Kristie. Don't go worst-case.* She couldn't change the past, but this time *she* was responsible for bringing these soldiers back to their families. Alive. All of them.

Heroics time is over. Please hightail your butt to the LZ so I can do my job.

A flash of light glinted through the dense wall of trees north of her position. "Was that movement at our twelve o'clock?" she asked Josué.

He studied the jungle in front of them. "I only see trees."

"Watch the area at my twelve," she ordered her gunner. She kept the location in her peripheral vision as she surveyed the area to her three o'clock, praying for their other friendly to emerge from that direction.

They had to get down and back up faster than a Hellfire missile. She hovered the aircraft to evaluate the landing zone. Most combat missions on her tour in Afghanistan involved desert landings in open spaces. She could execute those in her sleep. But jungle landings required more precision—and more time.

Time they didn't have.

"Heading down."

She pushed the stick, descending as rapidly as she dared. Before the craft even touched down, men in familiar US Army camouflage raced from the jungle's cover toward the bird. Four men carted a stretcher between them. Behind them, a robust soldier carried a slight figure over his shoulder fireman style. Slender, bare legs extended below a blue plaid skirt.

She maneuvered to give the soldiers a safe, straight-in approach to the aircraft's open side. The moment it touched down, her crew chief jumped out. Kristie scanned the clearing's perimeter. "Thirty seconds and we dust off."

Movement ahead yanked her attention to where an oversized black SUV came to a hard stop just past the tree line. The doors burst open, and four men emerged, all taking aim with automatic weapons. *Shit!*

"Tangos at my one o'clock!" Her pulse pounded in her ears over the engine noise, but her hand remained steady on the stick. An American soldier holding the back of the stretcher stumbled as they neared the craft. A dark circle formed and spread on the sleeve of the arm that now dangled at his side.

Her gaze shot from her fellow soldiers to the cartel gunmen. She didn't dare rotate the aircraft, but there was no way her gunner could fire at the attackers from his position—and someone had to.

Adrenaline surged through her. She popped her safety harness buckle. "You have the controls," she ordered Josué.

"Wh—" Josué started, but she tugged out her communications line before he confirmed the order—or called her loca.

Training took over, and she wrestled the M-4 from the mount next to her seat. Josué reached to stop her, but she ducked out, her elbow slipping through his grasp. She stuck close to the door for cover, raised the weapon's butt to her shoulder, and fired a burst of rounds at the vehicle.

Everything happened in slow-motion. The tug on her arms and the bounce of the muzzle as she barely squeezed the trigger.

The short-haired, slender tango near the front, passenger side of the vehicle jerked, then clutched a hand to his stomach. She could make out dark red blood staining his light-colored shirt and seeping over his fingers before he collapsed to his knees, then fell forward.

A gunman in a plaid shirt and jeans came around the door and knelt at the injured man's side. He fired at the aircraft again, then began pulling the wounded man back in the partial cover of the door. A short, stocky gunman darted around the back of the SUV, lifting the legs of the wounded man as they loaded him into the back seat.

From behind the relative safety of the hood, the driver stopped firing long enough to take in the men frantically motioning to him. He shoved the rear door closed, then climbed back in the driver's seat. With the passenger door still wide open, the SUV snaked back into the cover of the forest.

Her breath came in ragged gasps as she held her position and fired shots near where the vehicle had disappeared. Her gaze swept the tree line. In her peripheral vision, the soldier carrying someone deposited his load to the ground. His broad back blocked most of her view, but Kristie caught a glimpse of his passenger's long, dark hair. The woman scooted into the craft's belly before the soldier crowded her further in.

The operators hoisted the stretcher inside. The soldier who'd just been shot dove in, wincing in pain when he rolled out of the way. The remaining three operators spun to cover the area. Kristie climbed in, plunked down into her seat and secured her weapon. A bullet hit the nose of the aircraft. She flinched, and Josué ducked to the side. *Son of a bitch.* These guys didn't quit. Neither did the operators who unleashed a storm of return fire.

By the time she got buckled in, there was only the sound of the Black Hawk's blades and engines. The operators switched to handguns. If they were out of ammo, it was time to get the hell out of Dodge. With shaking hands, she jammed in the plug for her headset, missing whatever Josué said.

The last of the operators scrambled aboard.

"They all in?" she asked.

Josué jerked on the controls and lifted into the sky. His rapid ascent tilted the nose up before leveling the craft and rotating for the gunner to lay down fire at any remaining enemy.

"Hold up!" The choked voice of her crew chief, McCotter, sent a chill through her body.

Kristie glanced into the body of the aircraft. The linebacker-sized operator leaned down to speak directly into McCotter's headset.

"I still have a man down there. We are *not* leaving him behind." The deep, unmistakable voice of Ray Lundgren enunciated each word.

Oh, God, no. No!

"You said all in." Josué's voice hinted at panic. He didn't change course.

"We're going back."

"Bad idea." Josué shook his head. "Herrera very powerful. Has weapons to shoot us down. The cartel leaves no survivors."

She was *not* leaving a man behind. No way. Kristie reached for the stick. "I have the controls."

Josué maintained his grip rather than acknowledge the requested handoff. Kristie's pulse throbbed in her ears, dulling the roar of the turbine engines and the *thwack, thwack, thwack* of the blades slicing the air.

She checked her passengers. A shell-shocked teenage girl cowered in a protected posture between the soldiers flanking her. Their resolute faces locked on Kristie. The massive frame of the Special Ops team leader still loomed over McCotter. She knew Lundgren. Knew his family. If Eric had continued serving under Chief Lundgren, her husband would likely still be alive today.

Save herself and others or leave a man behind to certain death? She didn't have to take orders from Ray.

In that second, she knew what she had to do. The price might be her career, but better to take the risk than live with the knowledge she'd left a man behind. "Hang on, everyone." She leaned into Josué's field of vision and gripped the stick. "I. Have. The. Controls."

***

WANT TO KNOW WHAT HAPPENS NEXT? You can read the whole story of Kristie Donovan and Mack Hanlon in *Deadly Aim*.

ACKNOWLEDGMENTS

I remember having crushes on boys and celebrities as early as second grade. I think that's fairly common. Over the years, I would spin stories and add characters to television shows, usually imagining myself as the love interest of my current celebrity crush. I thought everyone's mind worked this way. Rather than study English or creative writing in college, my dad said I should study business or accounting to get a job when I graduated. So, I did. I worked in banking for a while before changing gear—and careers—to full-time mom. I did a variety of crafty things and created elaborate scrapbooks filled with pictures, an occasional poem and details I wanted to remember.

But I still dreamed up stories and came up with one I couldn't get out of my head. It wasn't based on a show or movie—though I envisioned it as a movie. I kept developing the plot and characters and eventually started writing it down. At first, I didn't tell anyone what I was doing. Then, I decided the best way to achieve my dream was to claim it. I told people the story—and they listened. No one laughed. Some read the completed script, and their comments and praise encouraged me to learn more about the craft of writing. Thank you to all those early supporters. Especially long-time friends, Lisa and Cindy, who called me the same week and said the same things about the script, and both concluded with: "I'd love to see this as a book."

The longest thing I'd ever written was a ten-page term paper. I knew I could tell a compelling story, but I had a lot to learn when it came to how to write a story. I like to compare writing to playing an instrument, in that no one wants to hear you when you are just starting. My apologies to my earliest readers! I didn't know how much I didn't know about writing. But thanks to joining a national writing organization, I had access to speakers, online classes, and workshops. I found critique partners – the BBTs, and I entered contests and got feedback from judges. My writing improved thanks to all the generous teachers and judges who gave of their time and expertise.

It's taken a lot of work to get here, but I've had fun along the way and made many wonderful friends. Thank you to the military troops I've supported, to other writers and preliminary readers, and my Golden Heart sisters: the '15 Dragonflies, '16 Mermaids, '17 Rebelles, '18 Persisters, and the '19 Omega class. Thanks especially to all my writer friends who've shared their insights, recommendations, and experiences related to indie publishing, so I'm not doing it by myself.

Thank you to my developmental editor, Holly Ingraham, for helping me see what was missing in the story. To my friend and copy editor, LTC Kathryn Barnsley (USAF Retired,) thank you for your service to our country. And thank you for keeping me out of I-still-can't-use-hyphens-correctly jail and for your invaluable perspective in ensuring I portray my military characters and their families (they are heroes, too!) respectfully and accurately. My stories wouldn't be the same without my main go-to guy for military and Special Ops information—MSG Dale Simpson (US Army Ret.) Thank you! Any errors are my own. Thanks to retired Detective Darrell Price for your expertise with criminal investigations during the timing of this novella. Thank you to Christy Hovland for her fabulous job creating a swoon-worthy cover. To JJ Kirkmon, Arlene McFarlane, and Pennie Leas for using your super proofing powers to catch errors and missing commas and tighten up my writing. JJ, you went above and beyond!

A special shout out to my critique partner and writing retreat cohort, Paula Huffman, who has read every version of everything I've written. You rock! We need more beach trips! Also, thanks to my writing meet-up buddies who answer the "What's another word to describe ...?" questions and keep me moving in the right direction when I would be tempted to play Bejeweled or check Facebook. I love our time together.

Most of all, THANK YOU to all my family and friends who've celebrated my successes along this journey. Not only can you say you "knew me when" but you still know me, and if you're reading this, thank you! I hope to see you and give you a hug.

ABOUT THE AUTHOR

About the Author

Tracy Brody has written a series of single-title romances featuring the Bad Karma Special Ops team whose love lives are as dangerous as their missions. A SHOT WORTH TAKING and IN THE WRONG SIGHTS won the Golden Heart® for romantic suspense in 2015 and 2016. DEADLY AIM was a four-time finalist in the Golden Heart.

She has a background in banking, retired to become a domestic engineer, and aims to supplement her husband's retirement using her overactive imagination. Tracy began writing spec movie and TV scripts, however, when two friends gave her the same feedback on a script, saying that they'd love to see it as a book, she didn't need to be hit over the head with a literal 2" x 4" to get the message. She joined RWA® and developed her craft and learned how to use commas correctly—most of the time.

Tracy lives in North Carolina where she and her husband are soon-to-be empty nesters. She has a daughter about to graduate college and a son who's living his dream as a software engineer in Silicon Valley. She has a sense of humor and is not afraid to use it. When not on a writing retreat with friends, she enjoys walking in her neighborhood, the park, or especially at the beach talking to herself as she plots books and scenes.

You can connect with me on my website:
https://www.tracybrody.com/
Sign up for my newsletter at https://www.tracybrody.com/newsletter-signup if you'd like to hear more about the Bad Karma Special Ops team and upcoming projects.

facebook.com/tracybrodyauthor

twitter.com/TracyBrodyBooks

instagram.com/tracybrodybooks

bookbub.com/authors/tracy-brody

ALSO BY TRACY BRODY

DEADLY AIM

Coming in March 2020

Widowed Black Hawk pilot, Kristie Donovan is determined not to fall for Mack Hanlon, the Special Ops sniper she saved on a mission tied to a drug cartel. Army regulations about rank mean Mack is off limits. Besides, she is not risking losing her heart to another man in Special Ops. Only when Mack insists on protecting her from a fellow soldier with a grudge, he rekindles her desire and hopes for love and a family.

Mack's marriage failed because his ex-wife was done with all things Army. However, the brave Black Hawk pilot who pulled off the daring rescue could be the woman who understands his drive to serve and support his career. She's also attractive and her interactions with his daughters have him on a mission to break through her excuse about the danger to their careers from engaging in a romantic relationship. Just when potential victory is in sight, they learn the drug cartel is targeting her as she is the only link to finding the men behind the mission that led to his son's death—Mack's Bad Karma Special Ops team.

Though Mack and his team are determined to protect Kristie, she has her own plan. Deploying to Afghanistan will keep her out of reach and keep Mack, his daughters, and his team safe. But when the cartel uses a ruse to capture Kristie before she can deploy, Mack and the team will have to find and save her from the drug lord hell bent on getting vengeance against them.

Bad Karma has never
felt so worth it.

DEADLY
AIM

AWARD-WINNING AUTHOR
TRACY BRODY

Made in the USA
Columbia, SC
02 July 2020